Roser Park

WENDY DALRYMPLE

Wendy Dalrymple

ROSER PARK

Chapter One

Chapter One

March 24, 1913

I am not well. I feel more and more trapped every day. This horrid house that my father built is more of a cell than a home. My thoughts are addled, and worst of all, Martin continues to insist that I see him. How many times can a woman say no? He becomes even more impertinent when father is out of town. His forward way with me is scandalous, and I can't help but feel for his wife. What must she think? I suppose I'll continue to rebuff his advances for as long as I can manage.

Martin says that he wants me to sit for a portrait when I am feeling better. He says that my beauty should be preserved forever on canvas. What a silly idea. No one sits for oil paintings anymore, it's so old-fashioned. My father will likely agree and force me to do it just the same. He never tells the good doctor no.

There are even more unsettling things on my mind than Martin and his unwanted advances; I saw the strange woman in the window reflection today. Mother says not to speak of it, but I have no one else to talk to, so I must write my thoughts and dreams down here. The woman looks so sad and lovely. It's as though she's trying to tell me something. But that's just me being silly again, isn't it?

Despite all my worries and the heat coming early this year, I try to keep my spirits up by reminding myself that things will be better in the fall. George will return from England, and we can truly start to plan our lives together. When we begin construction on our own home after the wedding, I hope we break ground far, far away from Roser Park. Yes, life will be better once George is home again. It must be.

Chapter Two

Chapter Two

A balmy, late summer breeze kissed Charlotte Slater's cheek as she approached the rambling blue and white century-old home at 684 Roser Park Drive. The estate — much like all the other neighboring homes — was nestled high up on a hill, tucked away behind a jungle of lush green fronds, exotic foliage, and colorful flower beds. Late summer sunlight dappled through overhanging oak branches against the clapboard siding of the two-story craftsman in a dancing, hypnotic display. A flock of ibis preened themselves along the banks of Booker Creek and somewhere in the distance the shrill cry of a limpkin broke through the afternoon tranquility. The creek itself was a decorative feature, a force of nature contained on all sides by man-made walls, dividing where the city ended, and the security of suburbia began. The bubbling body of water sliced through the historic neighborhood, cutting the residents of Roser Park off from downtown St. Petersburg, FL in a pristine and almost jarring way.

As Charlotte approached her destination, a hair-dryer warm wind whipped through the overhanging oaks, causing drapes of Spanish moss to shudder from their boughs. The real estate listing for 684 Roser Park Drive proved that the home she would be tending to for the next few weeks was a dream. The million-dollar property was brimming with architectural beauty, history, and mystery, things she had always appreciated, even as a young girl. It was the kind of house she would have wanted for herself if that sort of thing weren't completely out of reach. However, through a stroke of luck, for the next twenty-one days, if she were lucky, Charlotte could fantasize that she actually lived in the highly sought-after neighborhood near the bay. Three weeks of blissful silence and solace in an elegant, scenic home was exactly what she needed.

The online advertisement she had seen that very morning specifically stated that the house and dog sitting position would be ideal for a college student, which Charlotte most certainly was. At thirty-seven, she was perhaps not the typical kind of college student that the homeowners had in mind to hire, but she was enrolled in nearby University of South Florida's online nursing program just the same. Studying in the spare bedroom of her sisters' noisy, hectic home hadn't been easy the past few months, though she was grateful to have a soft place to land for the time being. Still, the prospect of having an entire house — and a gorgeous one at that — all to herself was enough to make her instantly answer the ad. The fact that she would be getting paid well on top of it all practically sealed the deal.

Charlotte smoothed a coppery strand of hair behind her ear and threw her shoulders back as her sneakers padded on the brick road beneath her feet. The bus stop was a quarter of a mile from the Roser Park neighborhood, and her feet suffered the effects of the journey as the scalding August asphalt burned through the thin soles of her shoes. After only a minute of walking, her thighs burned, chafing together in hot, prickly patches as they always did in the hottest part of summer. Sweat beaded on her upper lip; trickled down her back as the bright sunlight kicked back up from the road in radiant waves. Her destination was an oasis in the sprawling suburban desert.

The stone stairs lead to an impressive wraparound front porch, and the unmistakable feeling of someone watching clawed at her back. The meticulously kept estates in the neighborhood were all hewn close together, with little side yard space to speak of. Spying into another neighbor's front yard in Roser Park was just as easy as a turn of the head. It was this close, neighborly proximity that caused her to lock her gaze with a pair of dark irises peering from over a box hedge.

A long set of clipping shears glinted against the sun as the owner of the staring eyes snipped and pruned the yellow and green shrubs that cleaved the properties. An electric shock of adrenaline spiked down her chest all the way to her toes at the sudden realization that someone was staring at her. Charlotte narrowed her eyes into two suspicious slits at the baseball-capped stranger that continued to size her up as she made her way up the stairs toward the wooden glass-inlaid front door. Her heart had already been skipping at an erratic pace in anticipation of her job interview, but now it was positively leaping out of her chest.

Before she had a chance to fully collect herself and knock, the front door opened to a duo of enthusiastic, smiling expressions. The unfamiliar faces stared back at her like a pair of overeager twins, each sporting perfectly white-capped teeth set against tanned, mature skin. The homeowners wore sleek, fair hair cropped short and dappled with just a touch of silver. The man and woman both featured trim figures that hinted at regular exercise, organic groceries, and good health insurance. They wore minimal jewelry and outfitted themselves in crisp T-shirts and loose khaki shorts that were probably from Nordstroms, and not off the sales rack. Mr. and Mrs. Collier effused the very epitome of the Florida lifestyle that all the retirement communities want to sell to prospective snowbirds. Wealthy. Conservative. Immaculate.

"You must be Charlotte." The woman at the threshold cooed and extended a hand, "Judy Collier. Please, come in."

"Hi. Charlotte Slater." She accepted the woman's reach as a cool blast of conditioned air spilled out of the doorway.

The woman's hand was icy to the touch, soothing

and cool as the frigid interior. "This is my husband, Garrett."

Charlotte smiled and extended her reach to the man.

He hesitated; his mouth pursed in a thin line before speaking again in an authoritative voice reminiscent of an old Southern lawyer. "Are you sure you're at the right place?

Charlotte's eyes grew wide and darted to Judy's face. Her throat dried as she stammered out a response. "I . . ."

"Oh, *stop*." Judy slapped her husband on the arm. "Gary is such a kidder. Come on in."

Charlotte emerged into the foyer of the blissfully air-conditioned room, grateful to finally be out of the humidity and sun. Apart from a few modern amenities, the furnishings and decor of the interior appeared to be just as old as the foundation of the Roser Park house itself. A time capsule. The soft, muffled yip of a small dog echoed across the hardwood floor as the door closed behind her.

"I know the sitting room looks a little stuffy and old-fashioned." Judy waved her hand in the air, motioning for her to follow. "We started to renovate and tried to keep the home historically accurate but once we got to the kitchen? Forget it."

"I keep asking Judy if I can bring in a recliner and flatscreen, but I guess this room is just for show." Garrett chuckled.

Judy shot him a stern, but playful look, then pursed

her lips and sighed. "Have you house-sat much before, Charlotte?"

"Hmm?" Charlotte blinked and her already sun-warmed cheeks flushed. There was so much to take in from the thick, woolen carpet and heavy tropical print drapery to the decorative molding that lined every ceiling, wall, and floor. After only a few moments of being immersed in the home, she was already entranced. However, it was the portrait hanging over the fireplace of a woman dressed all in white with coils of strawberry blonde hair that had truly caught her attention. The subject of the painting pulled an unreadable expression and stared back at her in a muted, Impressionistic blur. The backdrop of the painting was clearly Booker Creek with its winding seawall and drooping, moss-laden oaks, only from a time before vehicles and streetlamps lined the brick paved road.

After a moment of silent staring, Charlotte snapped back down to earth, turned her attention to her would-be employer and forced a smile. "Yes. I've done a number of house-sitting jobs before. Babysitting and pet sitting too. I brought my references."

"I see you've spotted Mary Mueller." Judy paused. "Lovely portrait, isn't it?"

Charlotte nodded. "Someone from your family?"

"Heavens no." Judy waved in the air. "But the painting did come with the house. I believe the original homeowner may have even painted it."

"Did she live here then?"

"Apparently, she lived next door." Judy continued,

her slides *clomp, clomp, clomping* across the floor. "Mary Mueller was the daughter of the original home-owner at 682, some millionaire cookie baron or the other. He founded the neighborhood, apparently."

"He was madly in love with her." Garrett sighed; a sly smile spread across his flushed face.

"Who?" Charlotte's gaze was still locked on the ever-changing expression on Mary Mueller's face.

"The artist, of course." Garrett's voice was soft and dreamy. "Look at how he painted her."

"Oh, we don't know that!" Judy made her way toward the kitchen, her leather slides continuing to slap against the original hardwood floor.

Garrett shrugged. "It does make for a nice story when we take folks on a tour of the grounds."

The sitting room gave way to a narrow hallway as Charlotte followed Judy toward the back of the house. Garrett chuckled at her back and followed closely behind, almost boxing her into the claustrophobic, tight space. The floor creaked under their footsteps as she scanned the dark walls lined with old photos, paintings, and a long, horizontal mirror. Finally, the dark hallway opened to a bright, open space so full of light it was nearly blinding.

"Wow." Charlotte shielded her eyes, blinking against the bright, massive kitchen. Unlike the stuffy front entry brimming with heavy furniture and shrouded in heavy curtains, the kitchen was wide open and full of light. The whitewashed cabinets, delicate veined gray Carrara marble counters and stainless appliances were all new, but like the front of the house, the rest of the decor seemed to be from another era. The most impressive aspect of the kitchen, however, was the entire back wall constructed in floor-to-ceiling windows that looked out upon a terraced garden. The backyard offered even more lush foliage than the front, and to her utter relief, the patio also opened out onto a small, well-kept swimming pool.

"You said you had references?" Judy slipped on a pair of reading glasses as they reached the kitchen island.

"Oh! Yes." Charlotte reached into her tote bag and pulled out a folder that held her resume as well as a reference sheet of names and phone numbers of people she had worked for recently. In the last year she had done quite a bit of house-sitting, babysitting and dog sitting. It wasn't steady work, but it had been enough to get her through a rough patch.

Judy scanned the document and silently mouthed the names of her past employers as she read. Charlotte stopped herself from tapping her foot on the original black and white tile flooring as she scanned the kitchen.

Garrett whistled to himself and shuffled to the fridge. "Can I get you anything, Charlotte? Water? Coffee? Gin and tonic?"

She forced a smile. "Water would be great."

"I know that the ad specified a non-married, non-smoker, but I have to ask." Judy arched an eyebrow and pursed her lips. "No smoking, right?"

"Not at all." Charlotte gritted her teeth.

"And your health?" Garrett extended a bottle of Evian to her.

"Excuse me?"

"We just want to be certain that you're fit and feeling well." Judy batted her eyelashes and cocked her head to one side. "We don't mean to be personal, but we would hate to have to cut our vacation short because you fall ill from some underlying condition."

Charlotte's ears flamed. Cubicle life had been a living hell before she left her old job and her old life behind, but at least in the corporate world, employers couldn't ask personal questions. Often, questions and concerns regarding her health were insinuations that she could stand to lose a few pounds. Still, she reminded herself of the money and the freedom that this walk-in-the-park gig would allow her. The Collier's clearly were *not* nice people, but they were offering her attractive means to an end.

She sucked in her stomach and forced a smile. "I'm fit as a fiddle."

"Well, this all looks wonderful." Judy smiled up from the reference sheet. "I must say though, when we put out a call for a college student, I was expecting someone a little, well, *younger.*"

Charlotte frowned, unable to control her facade any longer. The Collier's were testing her to her limit. She took a long, deep pull of water to try and mask her rage.

"I'm sorry dear, what I mean to say is that it will

be nice to have a more *mature* house-sitter for once."
Judy grinned and pushed her references aside. "The
last time we tried to leave town, the neighbors said
the young woman we hired had a party."

"Oh, I wouldn't do that." Charlotte nearly choked
on her water. "That's just unprofessional."

"Of course, she left the house in order." Garrett
shook his head. "We didn't see any evidence of a party,
but we're still a little gun shy. You understand."

"Mmm, especially because of Laurence." Judy nodded.

Charlotte's eyes grew wide. "Laurence?"

"Our Yorkie. I'll bring him out to say hello in just a
moment. He's a sweet boy, but he's old and I need to
have someone I can trust to be sure to follow his diet
and give him his special food and medicine."

"Mrs. Collier, I can assure you I would take excellent care of your dog." Charlotte's jaw was beginning
to ache now from clenching.

"Please, call me Judy." She smiled and patted the
top of Charlotte's hand. "I'm *sure* you'll do an excellent job. This is why we wanted to meet in person
first. Garrett and I like to get a feel for someone's
personality before we hire anyone new."

A fresh bead of sweat formed at her brow despite
the brisk, piped-in air. Charlotte had only been inside the house at Roser Park Drive for five minutes
and was already getting run through the ringer. Her
senses were overloaded, and everything from the slap
of sabal palm leaves against the back kitchen window

to the slightly sweet and musty odor that permeated through the laundry detergent-scented air were heightened. The kitchen seemed brighter than ever as she held her breath, wondering what awful, insensitive thing they would say next.

"So, do I have the job then?"

Judy and Garrett glanced at one another.

Garrett sighed and scratched his head. "We would need you to start tomorrow. Would you be able to do that?"

"Of course." Charlotte nodded. "I can be here first thing in the morning if you need me."

"No need." Judy offered a reassuring smile. "Our flight doesn't leave until the evening. We'll just call a few of these references tonight to be sure, if that's alright with you?"

"Not a problem at all." Charlotte's eyes flicked to the ceiling as she calculated what she stood to make from the job. Five hundred dollars a week times three weeks; she would have just enough cash saved for the first and last month's deposit on her own apartment. By this time next month, she would be able to move into her own place if all went well. *Finally.*

"We'll just introduce you to Laurence now." Judy rose from her seat at the bar. "Then you'll already be friends when you come back tomorrow."

Judy disappeared into the hallway while Garrett moved over to a wet bar stationed in the corner of the kitchen. By the time he had poured himself two fingers of gin, Judy returned from the hallway with a feisty-looking caramel and gray Yorkshire Terrier under her arm.

"Oh, he's so sweet." Charlotte scratched the dog around the ears. "What kind of care does he need?"

"Well, he's on a special diet." Judy kissed the dog on the top of the head. "He's hypoglycemic and we have to be very careful of what he eats."

Charlotte relaxed a little as the dog licked her palm. "That's fine."

"We tried to board him once and it was just awful." Judy tsked. "Had to end our vacation in Cozumel early. We feel much better leaving him in his own home."

"Plus, we like for the house to stay occupied." Garrett chimed in. "We're so close to the south side, you know. Even with the alarm system, you can never be too careful about vandalism or break-ins."

Judy nodded in agreement as Charlotte bit down on her tongue. Hot prickles of angry heat flushed up her neck as she reminded herself again of the nice, fat check these not-so-nice people would be paying her. There was no point in arguing with these oblivious sycophants. Charlotte had heard negative talk about the south side her whole life, especially when she was growing up there.

"So, if you come back tomorrow around three, we'll give you the keys and show you the code to the alarm." Garrett smiled and downed the rest of the contents of his tumbler. "We'll leave a checklist on the counter here for you as well."

Charlotte swallowed her pride. Her face was still hot. "And when will you be back?"

"Just after Labor Day." Judy nodded. "We'll be in Rome and then Venice for a week, then we'll be on our two-week Mediterranean cruise."

"That sounds nice." Charlotte forced her millionth smile.

"Seems like we're all set then." Garrett clapped his hands together as he exited the kitchen. Judy followed with Laurence still curled up in her arms. Charlotte took one glance around the bright, cheerful kitchen. She nodded and followed the homeowners down the dark hallway again, imagining herself taking coffee at that very counter, her laptop open to her online college courses. This was going to be a good thing. It had to be.

"Oh, and there's one more thing." Garrett turned as he opened the front door. Golden afternoon sunlight spilled into the darkened front room, and for a split-second, the urge to run over the threshold and never return clutched at her gut. Charlotte ignored the impulse and forced yet another smile at her new employers.

"Our neighbor, Adam, will be over twice a week to care for the grounds. We take a lot of pride in our landscaping and in the summer, this damn grass grows so fast."

Charlotte glanced over as Garrett and Judy waved to the man next door. The glaring neighbor from before was still brandishing his large set of shears, only this time he was working on the far end of the adjacent yard. She blinked as a set of bronzed, glistening shoulders pivoted and turned against the late afternoon sun and the Collier's neighbor waved back at them. Adam of the silent, dark gaze and dangerous clipping shears wasn't wearing a shirt.

"That shouldn't be a problem." She shielded her face against the waning afternoon light. The sun blurred softly and hung lower now, and for a moment the sky seemed a little bluer, the grass a little greener. The parade of egrets and ibis that had been feasting on the lawn next door were gone and instead the drone of cicadas buzzed in the trees overhead. By the time Charlotte reached the bus stop near her sister's house it would likely be dark. She yawned, surprised as she glanced at the clock on her phone. It was summer and she should have had plenty of sunlight still, but time had gotten away from her somehow.

"Thanks again for this opportunity. This is the perfect place for me to get some studying done in peace."

"A mutually beneficial arrangement for all." Judy flashed her one last bright-as-the-sun smile. "We'll see you tomorrow then."

Charlotte nodded and shook their hands once more before taking off down the steps. She turned back to wave at the Collier's, but they had already disappeared inside the house. She frowned as she looked upon the Roser Park estate again, the historic house on the hill. Her own little slice of heaven for three whole weeks. She hitched her tote bag over her shoulder, shoved her hands deep into her pockets and walked at a brisk pace back down the brick road toward Martin Luther King Jr. Street. Even though she was happy about securing the easy money job, and completely romanced by the beauty of the old house, she couldn't shake the cold, unsettling sensation that settled into her core.

Chapter Three

Chapter Three

"Fifteen hundred dollars?"

Charlotte's sister, Emma, pulled up on the street in front of the house at Roser Park Drive the following day and threw her SUV into park. Her five-year-old nephew, Will, was fast asleep in his car seat, his plump little lips and chin dusted with crumbs. Eight-year-old Dakota had her nose buried in a paperback, her heavy home-cut bangs shrouding her eyes. Twelve-year-old Lacy had already been dropped off at soccer practice. Charlotte would miss her nieces and nephew, but she was more than ready for a break from being a full-time aunt and live-in babysitter.

"Yep." Charlotte leaned over and wrapped her sister in a hug. "I can finally afford to give you and Daryl your office back."

"I told you, there's no rush to move out." Emma rolled her eyes. "We have the room, and we love having you stay with us."

"I know, but *I'm* ready. It's time." Charlotte glanced over at the looming, historic home again. "I've never really lived alone. I'm kinda excited about the prospect of having my own space and my own things for once."

Emma jutted out her lower lip and gave her sister a half-smile, half-frown, her eyebrows still heavily knitted together. It was an expression that she knew to read as pity. She hated it, and hated the fact that she was getting used to it by now. "Okay then. If you need anything at all, just call us."

"I'm a big girl." Charlotte smiled. *"You're* the baby sister. I should be worried about *you.*"

Emma shrugged. "I know. I just worry. Another girl from the south side went missing just last week."

"I know. Rochelle. She was a freshman at my school." Charlotte sighed. "The news barely covered it. No surprise."

"I swear, I'm going to start my own podcast or something." Emma gripped her steering wheel and shook her head. "I couldn't imagine one of my kids just disappearing and no one giving two shits about it."

"Well, you don't have to worry about me." Charlotte grabbed her overnight duffle and laptop bag from the floor. She opened the back door, gave her niece a hug and blew a kiss to sleeping Will. "I'll be fine. See ya in three weeks."

"Not if I see you first." Emma smiled.

Charlotte slid the van door shut and waved as her sister pulled away from the Roser Park house back toward downtown. She hiked her duffle bag up on her shoulder, clutched her laptop case in her hand and plodded up the stairs of number 684 once again. The shirtless lawn maintenance neighbor was thankfully nowhere to be seen that day as she knocked on the front door, and yet, her eyes continued to dart into the yard next door in search of him just the same. Her mind drifted back to his dark eyes, and the long, metallic snips of shears against waxy green leaves. The rivulets of sweat that dripped down the valley of his tanned, well-defined back, glistening in the sun. Her breath hitched at the memory and just as she was about to knock again, the front door flew open, and she was met by Laurence's yippy bark.

"Garrett! The house-sitter is here!" Judy called.

Charlotte jumped and snapped her fist back down to her side as Judy opened the door. Judy was dressed in a smart lime green button-down blouse and white linen pants, her bob of platinum hair perfectly straightened. Laurence wriggled in her arms, panting, and yipping fiercely as Judy pivoted near two massive suitcases in the foyer.

"Sorry about Laurence." Judy motioned for her to enter. "He just *knows* when we are about to leave and becomes such a pest."

"It's okay." Charlotte stepped over the threshold and pressed her duffle to her chest. Judy continued toward the kitchen, and she instinctively fell in step behind her as the shadowy interior of the home enfolded her into its dark arms. They found Garrett seated at the counter of the bright white kitchen, scrolling through an electronic tablet with a notepad and pen. He looked up as they entered and smiled.

"Charlotte. So glad you made it." He rose to shake her hand. "I was just going over the controls for the security system and writing a few things down for you."

"Oh, that's great." Charlotte shifted her bag on her shoulders. "Is there somewhere I can put my things?"

"Of course." Judy placed Laurence on the floor. "I'll show you to your room and then give you a quickie tour of the house. We need to take off for the airport in about ten minutes though."

"That's fine." Charlotte followed Judy out of the kitchen with Laurence at their heels. The stairs to the second floor were located just off the kitchen on the other side of the long, dark hallway. Much like the foyer and the front entrance, the staircase was stuffy and old-fashioned, and featured an unusual, patterned wallpaper that snaked all the way up to the second floor. Green leafy ferns, vines and flower buds scrolled up and down in horizontal lines that were in stark contrast to the white banister and stair steps. The verdant wallpaper continued to the second-floor landing where they were met with an open landing that split off into two directions.

"Now our room is in the west wing. You won't need to go there." Judy waved toward the right side. "Your room will be here."

Judy grasped a faceted crystal handle knob on the first door to the left of the landing. A soft wave of afternoon light spilled through the crack in the wooden door, the rays dancing along the facets of the knob. A brilliant rainbow of sparkling light danced before Charlotte's eyes as the door opened to a musty, claustrophobic room. The space featured a gabled ceiling, and sharply pointed, triangular walls outfitted with even more dark green wallpaper. The room was sparse and decorated with a white rattan headboard on a full bed with a matching dresser, a vanity and little else. It instantly reminded her of a child's room. A haunted one.

"Is there a bathroom up here?" Charlotte entered the strange room and wrinkled her nose. She was immediately hit by a humid, musty wall of air, oppressive and heavy like a wet woolen blanket. It was considerably warmer on the second floor of the home, as multi-level homes in Florida tended to be. However, in the tiny guest room, the atmosphere was so stagnant and musty, Charlotte could scarcely breathe.

"There's a small guest bathroom right next door." Judy thumbed toward the hall. "I would suggest you use the downstairs bath though. It's more modern and has a claw foot tub."

Charlotte placed her bags on the bed and nodded. The room featured a single window that streamed in a soft wave of light overflowing with dancing particles of dust. The sun played through the window-pane onto the crystal knob and danced the sparkles of multi-color light into a darkened corner. The prism continued to play up the wall, swirling and dancing off the crystal knob. Charlotte narrowed her eyes as the light began to take a shape; iridescent eyes and lips smiled at her through the dark.

"I hope you won't be insulted," Judy tapped on her shoulder and paused, "but the rooms that we don't need you to access while we are gone will be locked."

Charlotte gasped and sucked in a ragged breath of air. Her body was rigid and heavy all at once as her eyes darted back to Judy. Surely, Judy saw the same thing?

"Gary has a lot of collectibles that he's very proud of, you see. We've had things go missing in the past. I hope you understand."

"No problem at all." Charlotte forced a smile at her seemingly oblivious employer. Her chest was tight as blood rushed to her ears. She glanced back at the corner; the room was cloaked in shadow again.

"Good." Judy chirped, her mauve lips spreading into a cheerful smile. "Let's head back to the kitchen then so Gary can show you how to use the security system."

Charlotte gratefully exited the strange little room, moving fast on her feet as though her very life depended on it. Judy clutched Laurence to her chest like a baby doll as they made their way down the stairs. A wide picture window spread across the front of the house overlooking the second-floor landing, no doubt the source of much of the upstairs heat. From her perch at the top of the staircase, Charlotte was able to get a perfect birds-eye-view into the neighboring front yard. The amount of wide, open and curtainless windows in almost every room in the house made her feel naked and exposed.

"I'm so sorry for the short house tour, but we really must be going." Judy released the Yorkie gently onto the floor.

"That's okay." Charlotte followed her back to the kitchen. "Does Laurence need to be fed tonight?"

Garrett rose from his seat, smiled, and handed her a red folder. "It's all here in the packet. The instructions for the security system are in there, as well as a few other useful things. Mostly just rules and instructions."

"Ready, dear?" Judy was already moving on swift feet toward the front of the house.

Garrett sighed and shook his head. "I suppose. Venice isn't going anywhere."

Charlotte followed Garrett down the dark hallway to the foyer to find Judy already halfway out the door. She still had so many questions, especially about the care of the dog, but the Collier's didn't seem to be half as thorough and particular about the house-sitting job as she had anticipated.

"Oh, Charlotte." Garrett snapped his fingers. "I nearly forgot. Be sure to keep Laurence away from the side of the house with the big flowering bush. It's our prized Datura and he loves to dig at the roots, the little devil."

"You got it, Mr. Collier." Charlotte nodded.

"Very good. See you in three weeks, then." Garrett

pushed the set of house keys into her hand, flashed a smile and took off behind his wife. The homeowners handed their overstuffed suitcases to the driver who was already waiting for them as Charlotte stood in the doorway, slightly unsteady on her feet. She raised her hand to wave goodbye as the car doors slammed shut, ignoring the cold, sinking feeling that crept into her gut again. The vehicle pulled away, leaving her and the dog all alone in the odd, empty old home.

Laurence whined at her heels, and against her better judgment, Charlotte bent down to pick the dog up. She scratched the lightweight, shivering Yorkie under the chin. "Well, Larry, it's just you and me and this spooky old house."

The dog yipped once more as she shut the front door and turned the deadbolt. She sighed and glanced down at the electronic tablet, folder and keys in her hand and headed to the kitchen in search of caffeine. She opened the cabinet doors one-by-one, taking stock of the pantry staples inside. To her delight, they did indeed have some coffee, though it was the instant, decaf kind. Charlotte didn't allow herself many luxuries these days, but good, strong coffee was one of them. The idea of not having her caffeinated crutch was almost depressing. A trip to the grocery store would have to happen sooner rather than later.

Charlotte heated a kettle of water just the same and got down to the business of reading up on the ins and outs of the historic home. She made a mental note to herself to hit the store in the morning for tea, groceries and some palo santo or sage to cleanse the creepy vibe from the Collier's house, though, in her estimation, a priest or a spiritual guide might be more in order.

The security system had been surprisingly easy to figure out, though the code 0684 was alarmingly easy to remember and too close to the house number for her comfort. According to the very basic instructions, Laurence wouldn't need to eat until six p.m. that night, so there wasn't much for her to do at the moment. Still, she located his stock of special diet food in the pantry and set it on the counter just the same. What she couldn't find was the dog's medicine.

She scanned the list that Garrett left, looking for directions on where to find the dog's medicine, but couldn't find anything. Charlotte opened the medicine cabinet, the refrigerator, and every drawer in the kitchen, but still found nothing. She made a mental note to call Judy and Garrett and ask where his medicine was and when he needed to have it. The high-maintenance little dog was the whole reason she was hired to stay there in the first place; if she couldn't even give him his medicine,

She returned to Garrett's list again, scanning the page in hopes of finding some clue about where to find the dog's medicine when her eyes rested on a different piece of information that piqued her interest. The neighbor, Adam, was scheduled to come by and work on the lawn on Mondays and Thursdays at nine a.m. She would have to remember to make herself scarce or run errands during those times. Laurence would also need to be walked once in the morning and once at night per their instructions, a task which Charlotte was actually looking forward to. She did a lot of walking these days and was excited to get a chance to take in the entire Roser Park neighborhood on foot. Other than that, the instructions said to help herself to whatever food she wanted and to be sure to dust, vacuum and clean up after herself. By all accounts, it appeared to be one of the easiest jobs she'd ever had.

Though the Collier's specifically stated that there were to be no visitors, Charlotte couldn't help but take a walking tour video of the home to send to her sister. Though she and Emma were vastly different from their appearance down to their personalities, one of the things they had discovered when she came to live with her sister was that they shared a love of DIY and home renovation. Charlotte fired up her old — but still very useful — smartphone camera and began to film.

"Hey Em, check this place out." She turned her phone camera to the rear-facing position, made a face at her reflection and turned the camera back around.

"So, this place is huge." Charlotte narrated, starting in the foyer. "Looks like all original hardwood floors and crown molding. Look at those cornices!"

Charlotte moved into the front sitting room toward the painting over the fireplace mantle. The somber-looking young woman in the portrait stared back at

her with a peculiar expression. "Check out this painting. Her name is Mary Mueller. Kind of looks like you,
huh?"

From there, Charlotte moved on down the hallway
toward the kitchen, making sure to take footage of the
giant mirror, framed vintage photographs and paintings that lined the narrow hall. When she reached the
kitchen, she eased open one of the glass sliding doors
forgetting that Laurence was at her heels. The little
dog slipped between her feet, bolted into the backyard, and took off after a squirrel.

"Shit." Her eyes darted around the back yard. "Sorry,
gotta go."

Every inch of the back yard was clustered with a
variety of dense, tropical foliage, blurring the property
lines from one house to the next. Her internal alarm
system kicked into overdrive as she realized he could
be just about anywhere. She ended the video tour,
stuffed the phone into her back pocket and sprinted
out onto the paved back porch and into the lush, me-
andering garden. A warm breeze whispered the honey
sweet scent of jacaranda blossoms through the air.
Still, there was no sign of the dog.

"Laurence!" Charlotte cupped her hand to her
mouth and called out into the silent, lush oasis. A terraced pathway led down to a small, tidy lot dominated
by a cerulean blue rectangular swimming pool flanked
with a mermaid statue on one side and a cherub on
the other. Twenty-five-foot-tall traveler palms fanned
out along the back edge of the property, while mango

trees on the left and orange and lemon trees on the right blocked out the sun. Thick rows of peach and coral colored hibiscus bushes hedged the property, creating a natural wall between the neighboring homes. It hadn't occurred to Charlotte that the Collier's wouldn't have an actual fence in their backyard to keep their treasured pet safe.

"Laurence!" It would be her luck that not even an hour into her house-sitting gig that the high-maintenance dog she was hired to watch would get lost. She fell into a light jog down the steps, hoping that she would find the Yorkie raising his leg against a bush or barking up a tree.

"Laurence!" Her pulse quickened as anxious vignettes of Laurence's tiny body under the wheel of a car flashed before her eyes. She didn't know the neighborhood at all and wouldn't have a clue where to begin looking for him. He wasn't responding to her call or barking anymore. He was probably across the street swimming in the creek for all she knew. Panic rose in her throat as she rounded the corner toward the front of the house. A dark cloud passed over the sun, sending shadows racing across the lawn as her heart hammered in her ears.

"Laurence! Oh!" Charlotte sped past the edge of the hibiscus bush in the direction she assumed that the dog had taken off in and nearly ran face-first into a set of shoulders. She gasped and gazed up at a pair of dark, furrowed eyes shaded from the afternoon sun by a frayed grass-stained baseball cap. It was Adam, of course, the leering yard maintenance neighbor. Only this time, he wasn't holding a set of deadly looking shears in his hands, but a shaking Yorkshire Terrier.

"Looks like Laurence got away again." The man stroked the top of the dog's silky head.

"You found him!" She cried and clasped her hands to her chest. "Oh, thank you."

"You're sitting for the Collier's." The words were more of a statement than a question. He pursed his lips together and the lines on his forehead deepened.

"Yes, I just started this afternoon . . ."

"You know you can't just let him out like that." His mouth was still screwed up into a frown. He reluctantly handed the dog to her just the same.

"I didn't mean to." Charlotte sniffed. "I didn't know the back yard wasn't fenced in."

"Hmph." The man grumbled and flicked his gaze at the sky. More dark clouds swept across the sun, shading his already hidden features. A summer rainstorm was blowing in from the direction of the nearby bay, bringing with it the smell of brine and earth and ozone.

"You must be Adam." She straightened her back and extended her hand. "I'm Charlotte. Charlotte Slater."

The man's hardened features grew slack as he glanced at her hand. He accepted her reach, his palms soft and warm against her own air condition chilled fingertips, a fact that she found pleasantly surprising. For someone that worked with gardening tools and tree branches all day, she was expecting a man like

Adam to have a hardened, calloused grip. They shook and he removed his cap, which sported the words "Mueller Maintenance" and a logo of a green lawn and setting sun. Sprays of silver at his temples and the crinkles at the corners of his eyes hinted that he was likely close to her age. She stared up at him, open-mouthed and utterly speechless and mused that perhaps she wouldn't have to make herself scarce on scheduled lawn maintenance day after all.

"Well, I'll let you get back to it." He released his grip on her and reached for one last scratch on Laurence's head. The dog whined and shook as the dark clouds rumbled overhead. "Looks like a storm's coming in."

Charlotte nodded in agreement and clutched Laurence to her chest. "Thank you for catching him. I promise it won't happen again."

Adam replaced the hat on top of his head and nodded. "G'night."

Charlotte stood there cotton-mouthed and dazed as he wiped his hands on his grass-stained jeans and gave her a casual wave goodbye. Laurence trembled in her arms again as another loud boom thundered in the distance. "Goodnight."

Adam disappeared through the thick wall of shrubs that separated the two properties, as though the barrier meant nothing to him at all. She and the trembling little dog were left alone in the shadow of the estate once again.

"That went well." She kissed the top of Laurence's head. He quaked and looked up at her with dark, sad eyes. "I was going to scold you, but maybe I should thank you."

Laurence whined again in response.

"Alright. Let's go get your dinner." She turned back toward the terraced patio steps as a fat droplet of rain slapped the pavers behind her. Charlotte hurried to open the back door and gently placed Laurence on the kitchen floor. By the time she fixed his supper a wall of rain was dumping outside, painting the backyard in a watercolor blur of shadowy green and blue dappled with distant pink and peach blossoms.

Still unnerved, she put on the teakettle and spooned out another acrid, disappointing serving of freeze-dried coffee. Coffee always had a way of helping her feel calm, from the ritual of preparing it to the fragrance and the way the warm cup felt in her hand. With her nerves completely shot, even her favorite hot beverage might not be enough to help at that moment. She tapped her fingertips on the countertop and waited for the water to heat, distracting herself instead with the memory of the unexpected meeting with her decidedly handsome neighbor.

Adam in the garden of Eden.

She snorted to herself at the insinuation as Laurence finished the last of his meal. Her stomach rumbled, reminding her that she hadn't eaten dinner yet herself. A quick rummage through the cupboards showed little more than an unopened box of crackers, a jar of olives and a can of tuna. Charlotte fixed herself another cup of decaf instant coffee and a regrettable pantry staple dinner, all the while day-dreaming about running into the curiously rough yet gentle groundskeeper. The idea of dating or romantic notions of any kind had been far from her thoughts in the wake of the divorce. With one look at Laurence safely nestled in his very capable arms, her long held defenses were easily giving way.

When she finished her sad meal, Charlotte rinsed the dishes, set the alarm on the house, and headed back upstairs to retrieve her things. There was no way she was going to spend the next three weeks in the odd, stuffy upstairs room. She would just as soon camp out in the dark, blissfully air-conditioned front sitting room. Even if her intended guest room wasn't hot and uncomfortable, she would have wanted to sleep downstairs. She always felt better in strange homes to be near an exit in case of a fire or natural disaster or something worse.

With her duffle, laptop bag, pillow and blanket at hand, Charlotte closed the door on the stuffy little room upstairs. The vintage tropical floral comforter she borrowed from the bed trailed behind her down the stairs like a wedding train down the stairs. Lightning flashed electric fingers through the wide picture window that opened up across from the second-floor landing as she descended the stairs. The distinct urge to move as fast as possible and away from the eerie second floor sunk into her gut as her feet skipped down the steps. At that moment, Charlotte knew that she would have no reason at all to climb those stairs again during her entire stay at the Roser Park house.

Laurence's nails tapped on the hardwood floor as she fluffed her pillow and spread the comforter on an overstuffed velvet sofa in the front room. It was seven p.m.; too early for bath and bed, and too stormy outside to do much of anything else. Even with all the time in the world on her hands, and a never-ending list of college coursework to do now that she was alone — really alone — Charlotte didn't quite know what to do with herself. She yawned and motioned to the dog, who responded by hopping up next to her on the couch and curling into a ball.

Charlotte pulled out her laptop and powered it on, hoping that the Collier's Wi-Fi instructions were correct. She smiled to herself as MuellerMaintenance-G5 popped up in the list of nearby internet access connections. She located JudyNGary-0864, typed in the pass code from the list of instructions and sighed with relief as her laptop connected. If she hadn't been able to get the internet access to work, the entire purpose of staying at the house to study would have been for nothing.

Despite her initial enthusiasm to dive into her studies, after a few minutes of glazing over course modules, her mind began to drift. She was wired but too emotionally and physically exhausted to really study now. Instead, she went into auto pilot and found herself diving into her various social media accounts and instantly regretting her decision. For months she had stayed away from all the usual suspects as she and Marcus went through the painful process of separating their lives. Old friends that they shared had either moved on or continued to keep in contact with him, which only served to reopen the wound of her failed marriage. The evidence of her old life continuing without her splayed across the laptop screen in smiling pictures at bars, the beach and baseball games still stung.

Disgusted, she clicked over to a streaming channel and settled in with a comforting sit-com instead. Cocooned in the folds of the plush couch and blanket, Charlotte sunk further and further down as the soft glow of the laptop shone in her face. Her head was fuzzy, and her vision hazed as the soft, familiar TV show lulled her, embracing her, and beckoning her to close her eyes. The silent, pale face of Mary Mueller stared down at her from over the fireplace mantle as she slipped off to sleep. Though she couldn't be sure, the expression of the woman in the portrait seemed to shift every time the painting was illuminated by flashes of lightning through the slits in the heavy curtains. She shook off the notion as the late summer storm continued to rage on, and before she knew it was fast asleep with Laurence curled up at her feet and the steady patter of rain thrumming outside.

Chapter Four

Chapter Four

April 1st, 1913

It's been far too long since I've heard from George. I'm beginning to worry that he's forgotten about me and that some sophisticated woman in London has caught his eye. If only I could have gone with him! The adventures we could have had! Though I am content here with my friends and my charity work, I can't help but want to run away from this place sometimes. Roser Park still doesn't feel like home, even a year later.

Martin isn't making things any easier. As I suspected, father agreed to let him paint the portrait of me. Every day starting this week I'll have to perch under the hot sun and sit stock still for a man that I despise. And for what? I don't even want a painting of myself. I can't wait to be free of this place.

The woman in the window continues to show herself to me. I was frightened of her at first, but now I feel a certain fondness for her. Why is she here? Who is she? Is she even real? I tried to speak to Lizzy and Emily about her, but my friends look at me so peculiarly that

I end up laughing it off. There is a woman in town that specializes in seances and the occult that may be able to help me though. I hope to take the trolly next week to meet with her. Perhaps she'll also have a way for me to hex Martin into leaving me be — haha!

Until next time Dear Diary . . . thank you for listening to my ramble of thoughts and strange ideas. I'm afraid you're the only one who will.

Chapter Five

Chapter Five

Charlotte's eyes flew open with a start at the sound of a gas motor roaring to life. The whir of blades tore through the silence of the morning as she rubbed her starry eyes and rummaged through a jumble of sheets. She plunged her hand deep into the velvet couch cushions in search of her phone, fingers probing through the layers of fabric. She finally located her device in the depths of the cushiony void and winced in the dark. The light from her phone made it even more difficult for her to focus on the characters displayed on the screen.

9:05 a.m. Shit.

Laurence circled at her heels, clearly in need of relief. She yawned and pulled herself up into a seated position as the shadowy living room around her tilted and reeled. Her tongue was wide and sandpapery in her mouth, her body crying out for water, just as it had done the morning before. Her still heavy eyelids struggled to blink open as she tried to orient herself, finally remembering where she was. The house in

Roser Park. The big, overstuffed sofa. The sweet little hypoglycemic Yorkshire Terrier that needed to pee and eat ASAP.

"Sorry, Larry." She stretched and forced herself to stand. "Let's get you outside."

Charlotte slipped into her sandals, picked up the dog and shuffled down the long, dark hall toward the kitchen. She frowned as she hooked Laurence's leash to his collar and poked her head out the kitchen door. No sign of a man with a lawnmower. She quickly realized that the whir of chopping blades was coming from the front of the house as she took Laurence down the terrace for a quick lift of his leg.

When Laurence was finished doing his business, she re-entered the kitchen and immediately downed an entire glass of water. Her head was still foggy, almost as though she had a really bad hangover even though she hadn't been drinking. She knew she wasn't feeling right; she didn't have to take nursing courses to know when her own body is reacting strangely. Still, she chalked up the persistent groggy sensation to the old house and Laurence's dander. Allergies affected her on and off, depending on the season or the environment, and clearly the Roser Park house was doing a number on her sinuses. Maybe she didn't need more coffee, but some allergy medication.

With the dog fed, Charlotte placed her cup by the sink, sucked in a deep breath and made her way down the dark hall again toward the front of the house. She knew it was wrong, and yes, technically *spying*, but she couldn't help but want to sneak another peek at Adam as he toiled under the early morning sun. She moved to the heavily curtained front windows and parted them ever-so-slightly, hoping that the darkened space would conceal her messy bedhead and pajamas as she essentially leered at the landscaper. To her utter disappointment, Adam and his lawnmower were just out of sight, down the sloping front yard hacking away at the high grass near the hibiscus bush hedge.

Charlotte had spent the better part of her first full day at the house on Roser Park Drive this way, studying, taking care of Laurence, and staking out Adam. It all started innocently enough when she went upstairs on her first morning in the house in search of hand soap in the guest bathroom. The wide upstairs picture window offered an excellent view of not only Booker Creek, but also of the front yard and the neighboring yard as well. It was there that she discovered the perfect place to catch an undercover glimpse of the landscaper.

She didn't mean to fall into voyeurism. In all fairness, Charlotte knew how important it was to give people their privacy, but the name "Mueller" on his work hat didn't strike her as a coincidence. If Adam lived next door and shared the same last name as the woman in the painting, it only reasoned that he could be related to her. Now, as the early Monday morning sun bathed her in warm light, Charlotte found herself at the top of the stairs watching him once again. If it weren't for the eerie sensation she got from simply standing at the top of the second-floor stairs, she could have happily loitered there watching him work all day.

He's probably married, she scolded herself. She shook her head and reminded herself of where she was, and that she should be professional. That she shouldn't be wasting her time appreciating the way his sweat had already begun to stipple the back of his white cotton shirt. She shouldn't be staring. Adam suddenly turned a sharp corner and faced the house, his work-hardened arms pushing the lawnmower in front of him through the carpet of tall grass. Before she could tear her eyes away, he lifted his head and — to her utter astonishment — stared up from under the brim of his hat and locked directly into her gaze.

Shit! Charlotte cursed under her breath and ducked out of view. The deep green vines of the staircase wallpaper snaked and shivered all around her as she crawled backwards down the stairs to avoid being seen. She had been caught. The lawnmower engine cut out and shortly after, three swift knocks on the front door confirmed her fears.

Oh shit, oh shit, oh shit.

Her adrenaline spiked as Laurence yipped and scratched at the front door. She hadn't even brushed her teeth yet and was still wearing her faded cartoon print pajamas. She smoothed her hair, shushed Laurence, and eased him out of the way of the door with her foot. Charlotte let out a long, slow breath and prepared herself for who she knew would be on the other side of the door.

"Everything okay?" Just like the other day, Adam was outfitted in his usual landscaping uniform of a white tee, jeans, heavy-duty boots, and a Mueller Maintenance baseball cap. A spray of sun kissed pink played out on the apples of his cheeks as he leaned against the door frame struggling to catch his breath. His freshly shaved, razor-sharp jaw glistened from the stream of sweat that poured from the wild, silver-flecked hair that jutted out from under his baseball cap in unruly angles. A red lawnmower stood immobile some one hundred yards down the slope of the steep yard. By her estimation, Adam must have sprinted uphill to the front door.

"I'm fine." She pulled her robe tightly across her chest. "Why wouldn't I be?"

"Oh, good." He exhaled heavily. "I'm sorry. I don't mean to pry. It looked like you might have fallen."

The heat in her cheeks flared into a full-blown blush. Not only had she been caught spying on him, but now she had to lie.

"Oh, that!" Her brain was still slightly foggy from her odd night of sleep, and the cheerful stream of sunlight that assaulted her eyes didn't help matters either. It wasn't the sun or her head that was truly causing Charlotte to stumble over her words though; Adam's sweaty arrival at the front door made her clam up like a self-conscious teenager.

"Yeah." She managed, smoothing her hair back

from her face. "I guess I'm not used to the stairs yet. Tricky landing."

"I hope my mowing didn't disturb you. Most of my clients are away this time of day." Adam removed his cap and ran a hand through his sweat-dampened hair, a thick set of keys dangling from a hook at his side. Her heart raced even faster as she rocked back on her heels. The entire outside world seemed to shimmer and pulse as he stared down at her. Charlotte had never fainted once in her life, and certainly not over a man, but at that moment, the very real sensation of passing out was threatening to overtake her.

"I'm sorry." She blinked away the stars in her eyes, her ankles wobbly. "I think I need to go sit down."

"Hey, are you okay?"

Before she could respond, Charlotte's hand slipped away from the door frame and her legs gave out beneath her. Adam's hands shot out to catch her, his fingers curling around the worn fabric of her pajamas just in the nick of time. He slid his arms underneath her and helped her to her feet, pushing her through the doorway and into the darkened front room.

"Let's get you over here." He shut the front door behind him with one foot. Laurence yipped and circled their ankles as he helped her to the velvety couch where her blanket, laptop and personal items were still spread around. If she hadn't been so lightheaded, Charlotte would have certainly been embarrassed about the state of herself and her surroundings.

"I don't know what happened." She rubbed her eyes. Stars still danced across her line of sight.

"Let me get you some water." Adam's footsteps, and the keys jingling at his side faded as he disappeared down the hall toward the back of the house. Charlotte sat up and her eyes flew to the portrait of Mary Mueller. The stoic figure seemed to stare back down at her as the stars subsided and her head righted itself again. Charlotte could sense the blood rushing back to her deadened limbs in sharp, painful waves. She glanced at the big, insipid eyes of the animated sheep on her pajamas and cursed herself for not packing a satin nightgown instead.

Heavy footsteps plodded behind her. She sucked in a deep lungful of air, trying to steady her racing heart. Adam handed her a glass of water and stood back as she took a grateful sip. The world was coming back into focus, as was an overwhelming sense of utter mortification.

"Thank you." She gripped the half-empty glass. "That's never happened before."

"It's pretty hot out." He wiped the sweat from his brow. "Maybe you're dehydrated?"

"I think it's just allergies." Charlotte hugged her arms to her chest. "Mold or pollen or something."

"Well, maybe you should see a doctor if it happens again?" He readjusted the brim of his hat. "Are you going to be okay?"

Charlotte pushed herself up off the couch and stood, more clear-headed than before. She scrunched her tingling toes against the hardwood floor and nodded. "I think so."

"I can call someone if you like."

Charlotte pursed her lips together as she assessed the enigma of the man that stood before her. She used to think that she was able to size people up from first impressions and gut instinct, but if the past year taught her anything it was that people weren't always what they seemed. This gruff landscaper might actually be a nice guy after all.

"I'll be fine." She offered her best reassuring smile. "I'm sure it was just a fluke."

"If you're sure, then I better get back out there." He smiled. "That yard isn't gonna mow itself."

Charlotte followed him to the door, still not entirely steady on her feet and internally dying of embarrassment. Getting caught staring was bad enough but looking like a vulnerable mess in front of a stranger was too much. Surely now she would never be able to show her face in the neighborhood. Surely...

"Oh, one more thing." He reached into his back pocket and pulled out a thick, worn leather wallet. He struggled for a moment, then fished out a small white card. "This is my business card. It's got my cell number on it if you need anything while you're here."

She held out her hand and he pressed the card into her palm. She exhaled slowly as she eyed the simple "Mueller Maintenance" card, the jumble of numbers dancing before her eyes.

"Mueller." She could swear color rushed to his

cheeks as she met his gaze. Maybe her sheep pajamas hadn't turned him off that much after all.

"You know, there's a painting of a woman with your last name in the living room."

Adam nodded; his eyebrows raised. "Yep. That would be my great aunt, Mary."

"I knew it." Charlotte's eyes widened. "So why is the painting here instead of hanging in your home?"

"It's an old story. My grandfather would have been able to tell you better," he sighed. "I guess the owner of this house was the artist. He had a little crush on her and wanted to keep the painting after she died."

"She *died*?"

"Yeah. She was young. It must have been right around the time her portrait was painted."

Adam's gaze wandered past her into the living room in the direction of the painting.

Charlotte's head whipped around to the portrait and then back at Adam again. "Do you know how she died?"

Adam shrugged. "I think they ruled it as natural causes. She might have had some undiagnosed mental illnesses too. I don't know, my family covered it up at the time."

"How awful." Charlotte folded her arms across her chest. "Well, thank you again."

"No problem. Feel better." Adam grasped the brim of his baseball hat and gave it a slight tip as he strode back out the door and down the front lawn toward his mower. Charlotte stood in the doorway of the house with Laurence at her heels and his business card hot in her hand.

She closed the door and set the alarm again as the sound of a lawnmower engine filled the air once again, still baffled at the exchange that had just happened. "What was that all about, Laurence?"

The Yorkie looked up at her with his mouth open, his nails tapping furiously on the hardwood floor.

"I obviously need coffee." She pulled her pajama top away from her, dipped her nose beneath the neckline and sniffed. "And a bath."

Laurence followed her down the dark hall to the kitchen, her stomach rumbling. She hadn't made breakfast for herself yet either. *Hunger.* Maybe that was her problem. Lack of food combined with her allergies and impending PMS must have been what caused her to get all lightheaded. With every passing year dizzy spells and a variety of other new bodily symptoms came with her shifting hormones, but she didn't like the sensation just the same.

Charlotte yawned and winced as she entered the bright kitchen again. She had a lot planned for that Monday and couldn't waste her time worrying about how she looked in front of the sweaty, frustratingly handsome landscaper. She needed to eat, bathe, walk Laurence, then had three study modules to do, and all before lunch. More of the Collier's crappy coffee was in order to get her in gear. As she went to the sink to fill the teakettle with water, something unusual caught her eye.

The kitchen featured a wide farm-style kitchen sink that had been empty and pristine that morning. Now two empty water glasses and Laurence's used food dish sat in the sink, waiting to be washed. A sick, stabbing sensation worked on her insides as she froze, her eyes trained on the dishes in the sink. She couldn't be sure of where she had placed her water glass that morning, but she was certain that she had left Laurence's food dish on the ground.

Adam. He must have put the dishes in the sink. But why?

Charlotte's shoulders tightened as she filled up the teakettle and tried to explain away the events of the morning in her mind. Something wasn't right, but then again, things always seemed strange at first when she was house sitting in a new place. She finished her toast and unsatisfying instant coffee that morning in unsettled silence, hanging on every creak in the old house, every blast of the lawnmower engine outside. She wrapped her hands around the warm mug; a morning ritual that usually soothed and grounded her. For whatever reason, there was no solace or comfort to be found at the bottom of her cup that day.

Determined not to let her imagination run away with her, Charlotte washed the dishes in the sink, set them in the drying rack and headed toward the downstairs bathroom to get cleaned up for the day. She had only showered in the home so far, and was eager to test out the big, luxurious claw foot tub that dominated the first-floor bathroom. Through the various interior design shows she had binged with her sister; she could tell that the downstairs bathroom had been another room at one time; perhaps a study or a second sitting room. It was a rather large space just off the kitchen and adjacent to the staircase, and far too big for most turn of the century bathrooms. Homes from its era that did have water closets or washrooms were typically tiny little boxes, but this bathroom was the size of a bedroom.

With her towel and a fresh change of clothes in hand, Charlotte ran the water in the tub and stripped off her pajamas. Even though the security system on the house was armed and the bathroom door was locked, she still couldn't help but feel exposed some-how in the massive space. She stepped into the scald-ing water and lowered her body beneath the surface, eager to hide herself somehow.

Her eyes trailed up as the water filled the tub; much like the rest of the house, even the ceiling was ornate. Intricate swirls were etched into the plaster above in a textured design that shifted and writhed in the steam. Her thoughts were fuzzy and lightheaded again. In that moment Charlotte was reminded of the time that the city water supply on the south side had accidentally been over chlorinated. A half dozen people became sick, and one person nearly died as the steam from their tubs and showers poisoned them. Maybe that was her problem. Chlorine poisoning. She dunked her head under the surface and made a quick job of scrubbing her body and washing her hair just in case. There would be no relaxing in the tub for her that day.

Charlotte's pulse raced as she unplugged the drain, wrapped herself in the towel and stepped out of the tub. Her gaze fell on the wooden closet door at the far end of the bathroom. It was the same kind of door that was in all the other rooms in the house, though unlike the other doors, this one was missing a crystal knob. The knob on the bathroom closet door seemed out of place and utilitarian, far too modern and heavy-duty for a bathroom closet. Though Charlotte suppressed the urge to snoop around too much in the big, creepy house, even she wasn't immune to her own curiosity. The Collier's were filthy rich after all, and Judy had mentioned collectibles and valuables. Surely though, the bathroom closet would only have towels, extra toilet paper and fancy department store face cream stashed away in there, right?

Still dripping, Charlotte padded over to the far side of the bathroom, careful to avoid her own reflection in the vanity. Though she wasn't ashamed of her body, it was still hard to look herself in the face these days. Starting over again wasn't easy. She was a failure in her professional life. A failure in her marriage. No amount of Pilates or hyaluronic acid could erase the fact that on the inside, she was ugly.

Charlotte pursed her lips as her eyes zeroed in on the heavy-duty closet doorknob. She wrapped her hand around its cool metal surface and turned, only to find the closet door locked. She scoffed to herself, not entirely surprised that the Collier's would lock up their extra soap and toilet paper. Apparently "use whatever you need" only referred to a few stale crackers and condiments in the kitchen. She exhaled deeply and added toilet paper to the mental list of supplies that she would need to pick up on her next grocery run.

With her pulse pounding, Charlotte dried off, slipped into a daisy print sundress, and wrapped her damp hair in a towel. The urge to leave the bathroom as quickly as possible pushed her to want to finish her routine and put on her makeup in the well-lit kitchen instead. For whatever reason, Charlotte suddenly couldn't stand to be in the bathroom one moment longer. As her grandmother would have said, it felt as if someone had walked over her grave.

By the time she reached the kitchen, the muffled buzz of the lawnmower through the walls had migrated from the front to the back yard. She eased into the stool at the kitchen counter with her makeup bag in hand and gazed out the wide back windows and onto the patio. In the distance she could clearly see Adam working on the small patch of grass by the side of the pool, pushing and pulling the lawnmower back and forth. She sucked in a quick, shallow breath as she realized that she was once again spying on her neighbor and landscaper. Makeup would have to wait. Fortunately, Laurence whined at her heels, reminding her that it was likely time to walk the little dog again.

She sighed. "Okay, Larry. Let me go grab my shoes."

Charlotte grabbed his leash from the hook while the little dog yipped and turned in circles. Suddenly a loud crash from the direction of the front sitting room cut over the faraway buzz of the lawnmower. Laurence stood stock still and pointed in the direction of the sound as a low growl escaped from his muzzle.

"What did you get into?" With the leash still in hand, Charlotte left the kitchen and plodded down the long hall toward the cool, dark front sitting room. It didn't take long for her to find the cause of the noise. There, lying in a heap on the ground, was her laptop, shattered to pieces.

Chapter Six

Chapter Six

"Yes, completely busted. Okay, the address is 684 Roser Park Drive, St. Petersburg. How long will it take? That's fine I guess. Thank you."

Charlotte pushed aside her useless device, tossed her cell phone on the couch, and rested her chin in her hand. Though her new laptop was thankfully still under warranty, as she suspected, it would be out of commission for almost a week. She slowly exhaled through her nose and considered her options; she could wait for her laptop to be fixed and get behind on her work. She could try and access her courses on her cell phone and pray that her ancient phone would work, or she could go downtown to the university library and use the computer lab. It didn't take much deliberation for Charlotte to decide that she already needed a break from the Roser Park house.

The library computer lab was only open until seven p.m. that day, so Charlotte knew that she needed to move fast. Laurence's evening walk would have to wait until later. She ran a brush through her hair, threw on a pair of jeans, her sneakers and a tee and locked up the house just as the Collier's had directed. With every step she took away from the house, her spirits seemed to lift. Whether it was the fresh air or the blood pumping through her veins, her mental fog seemed to lift by the time she stepped onto the city bus.

Charlotte settled into her seat on the bus and rested her pack in her lap. The image of her busted laptop continued to nudge at the back of her mind. She knew that she wasn't the most graceful person, but when it came to her belongings, she was typically careful. She especially babied her new laptop, a device that not only was the key to her educational future but something she couldn't afford to replace. She knew that she had placed the laptop far enough back on the couch cushions to be safe. How could it have ended up on the floor?

After a few stops, the city bus squealed to a halt outside of the waterfront college campus. Even though she took most of her courses online, she often visited the library to use the labs or the printer. The library was one of her favorite places on campus and featured secluded areas to study and stunning views of Tampa Bay. The sun hung low in the sky as she eased into a desk at the computer lab and got to work. Nearly three hours passed as she listened to lectures, caught up on modules and finished up a paper. By the time she looked up from her screen and stretched, the sun was gone from the sky and the computer lab was nearly empty.

Charlotte.

All the feeling left her legs as she snapped her head around. Even though she had her earplugs firmly in place, she could have sworn someone called her name. Her eyes trailed up the staircase to the second floor of the library just in time to catch a flash of a long, black skirt disappearing around the corner of a bookshelf.

She checked the time; 6:45. The library would be closing soon, and she was practically done with her work. She sighed and closed out her program, not looking forward to the long walk back to the Roser Park estate in the dark.

Charlotte.

Her gaze flicked to the second floor again. Someone *definitely* called her name this time. It wasn't a voice that she recognized, though it was one that felt familiar to her somehow. Against her better judgment, Charlotte slung her backpack over her shoulder and headed toward the library staircase. She didn't venture up to the second floor of the library often; it was where the non-fiction and reference books were kept. The second level was even emptier than the main floor, and as she ventured through the aisles, there was only the sound of her steady heartbeat and the thrum of the overhead fluorescent lights to guide her. Her head turned at the soft, swishing sound of fabric. Her nose and mouth filled with a heady aroma, the scent and taste of perfume and decaying flowers hung heavy in the air.

THUD.

Charlotte spun around. Waves of adrenaline flooded her body, her heart fluttering faster than ever. Her eyes darted up and down the aisles, and for a moment, the terrifying image of the floating librarian from *Ghostbusters* flashed through her mind. She turned on her heels ready to sprint for the staircase. But before she even took two steps, her foot nudged against something hard and heavy on the carpeted library floor.

She gazed down to see a thick, hardcover book bound in red and black leather, protected in the library's usual plastic overcover sleeve. Charlotte bent to pick up the heavy tome, unable to leave a book on the floor even in her distressed state. She blinked, her breath hitching in her throat as she read the title on the spine.

Roser Park: St. Petersburg's Gilded Age

Charlotte clutched the book to her chest, the thump of her erratic pulse pounding loudly in her ears. The buzz of fluorescent lights were even more intense as the sound of swaying fabric — taffeta or a heavy chiffon perhaps — grew nearer. She urged her dead legs to move and flew down the stairs with the book pressed against her hammering heart.

***

It was completely dark when Charlotte returned to the Roser Park neighborhood later that night. With no moon and only the pale light of the fancy, upscale streetlamps to guide her, Charlotte was even more creeped out than usual as she walked toward home. She was still unnerved by the events at the library, so much so that she had nearly tried to leave without checking out the book. The librarian gave her an extra dirty look on her way out, either from being one of the last one's there or because it looked like she was trying to steal materials.

After she left the library, Charlotte stopped by the school general store in search of good coffee and fresh fruit only to find that it was closed. Her only other option by bus or on foot was a nearby convenience store, but she was disappointed at the offerings they had. Charlotte did, however, pick up a pack of sage incense by the convenience store register to burn. She didn't know if she actually believed in ghosts or incantations, but she figured that it couldn't hurt.

The bus dropped Charlotte off at the end of the street near ten p.m. Roser Park was dark, silent and humid as she picked up the pace toward the house. The icky sensation of being watched crawled along the base of her spine as she hurried along the brick paved road, and Charlotte decided that she was definitely *not* going to be walking Laurence that night. She would make it up to him somehow, but there was no way that she could stand being out in the unfamiliar, spooky neighborhood after dark for another moment. If she had someone to walk with her, perhaps it would be different, but for whatever reason, the tingling sensation in her spine and the constant spike of adrenaline in her veins told her it wasn't safe.

The house appeared to be secure as she unbolted the front door and disarmed the alarm. Everything looked normal and quiet, save for the scolding yips of a spirited little Yorkie. Still, an uneasy feeling persisted as she fed Laurence and put on the teakettle. Simply being in the house kicked her equilibrium off kilter and made her body feel even heavier than usual, almost as though she were underwater or in a vacuum. It was a feeling she couldn't shake.

Charlotte rummaged through one of the kitchen drawers, located a lighter and lit the end of one of the sage incense sticks. She propped it on the edge of a ceramic plate and sipped her tea, and gazed out the back window. A light flicked on next door, illuminating the neighboring backyard and casting leafy shadows into the night. Charlotte pursed her lips, cut the kitchen light, and tiptoed to the corner of the room for a better view. She sighed as the shape of a man emerged in the dark with a trash bag in hand. Through the old thin walls, she could hear him singing again, another old rock ballad she remembered from her youth. Normally hearing people sing out loud was not appealing to her, but Adam had a nice voice, and there was something almost sweet and endearing about someone so gruff belting out songs about love into the night.

BANG.

Charlotte jumped at the sound, splashing hot tea

all over her hands. For what seemed like the millionth time that day, her heart leaped into her throat and her body froze. Laurence looked up at her and tilted his head to the side. She had locked all the doors and made sure that the house alarm was set, but those facts didn't reassure her at all. Charlotte mustered up whatever little bit of courage she still had, reached for a knife from the block on the counter and ventured toward the sound.

"The cops are on their way!" Charlotte threw her shoulders back and affected her most authoritative voice. Laurence's nails clicked behind her, unbothered. Surely, if there was an intruder in the house, the dog would let her know? "You better leave before they get here!"

Charlotte held the kitchen knife high in the air. Visions of masked men and demonic, pizza-faced nightmare stalkers flashed before her eyes. She was no tough-as-nails "Final Girl", but after the year of hell she had been through, Charlotte wouldn't go down easy either. She held her breath and ventured into the living room, ready to defend herself from whoever — or whatever — made the noise.

"Ah!" A figure jumped out at her from around the corner and Charlotte screamed again. She faced the outline of a woman backlit in a harsh, glowing light, her arm held high. Her soul nearly left her body as she realized that there was only a mirror in front of her at the end of the long hallway.

"You *complete* scaredy cat." She scolded herself and

shuddered a ragged breath as her eyes darted around the darkened, empty sitting room. There, on the patterned wool rug, was the obvious source of the loud, thudding noise. Her backpack had spilled over on the couch and the huge library book was splayed out on the ground, nearly in the same position as her laptop had been earlier that day. She frowned, still clutching the knife as an unworried Laurence followed at her side.

"Hmm. Maybe there's a dip in the floor here?" Charlotte reached over and picked up the book. She glanced down at Laurence as if he could answer. He only replied with an open-mouthed, toothy dog smile.

Charlotte turned the opened book over to where it had landed on the ground. Some of the pages had become bent in the process, and as she smoothed them out, a familiar image came into view. The photos inside the book were printed in black and white, but the house that stared back at her was easily recognizable. Same clapboard siding. Nearly identical tropical foliage.

"Look, Laurence. It's your house." Now a little more at ease, Charlotte set the kitchen knife on the side table and settled onto the couch. She brushed away any lingering worries of intruders lurking in dark corners and scanned the page. Much of the information was what she already knew; that the house was old and was built by some food manufacturer tycoon. She turned the page and another familiar image stared back at her. It was the same likeness that hung over the mantle.

Charlotte stared at the painting of Mary Mueller and then down at the replica of the portrait in the book. In black and white, the woman seemed even sadder somehow, her eyes hooded and dark, all the color gone from the flush of her cheeks to her green satin shoes. Staring at the picture simultaneously filled Charlotte with a deep sadness and an unmistakable feeling of dread. She read the passage under her image, her fingers trembling under the page.

Mary Mueller, daughter of cookie tycoon Horace Mueller, died in 1913 under mysterious circumstances. Her fiancé, George Dawson, also disappeared that same year enroute home to St. Petersburg from London. The Mueller family had also suffered the devastating loss of Mary's mother, Eugenia Mueller, earlier that year in a gruesome carriage accident. The Mueller family was said to be cursed when...

BANG! BANG! BANG!

Charlotte gasped again. Three swift raps on the front door snapped her out of her haze and launched her pulse and her anxiety through the roof. She reached for the knife again, tossed the book aside and rose to her feet.

"Hey! Everything okay in there?"

Charlotte lowered the knife and exhaled at the sound of Adam's muffled voice. She placed the kitchen knife back on the table and walked on shaky legs toward the entryway. Relieved but still on edge, she turned the deadbolt, slid the chain lock, and opened the door to Adam, his decidedly handsome features scrunched with concern.

"Hi." Charlotte smiled and hugged her arms to her chest.

Adam panted and glanced over her shoulder before meeting her gaze again. "I heard a scream."

"It was nothing. Something just startled me." Charlotte closed her eyes, shook her head, and gazed back at him with a half-smile. "You could hear me?"

"Yeah, I was just out going for a jog. Sounded pretty bad." Adam hitched his thumb toward the street. "Sorry. I didn't want to bother you; I was just worried."

"That's okay. I appreciate it." Charlotte nodded. She bit her lower lip as her eyes trailed down his form. Gray sweatpants. Blue and white trail runners. Fitted gray tee. For a split second she considered inviting him in. "Thank you."

"So, what was it?" He propped one hand on his hip and leaned against the door frame on his forearm.

Charlotte's brain momentarily stopped working. "What was what?"

"The thing... that made you scream?" He smiled.

Charlotte blinked again and remembered to breathe. "Oh! Ha ha. I'm just . . . jumpy. There was a noise. A book fell on the floor."

Adam smirked and nodded. "These old houses are creepy, especially when you're all alone. I kind of hate it."

"I know exactly what you mean." Charlotte licked

her lips. A cool wisp of early autumn breeze blew up the hill, bringing with it the aroma of decaying leaves and the brackish water of Booker Creek.

Adam glanced back toward the road and shoved his hands deep in his sweatpants pockets. "Well, if you're sure you're okay, I'll leave you to it."

"I'm good. Thanks for checking." She offered up a half smile. "Enjoy your run."

"G'night."

She closed the door and sighed as he disappeared down the stairs and into the night. For a split second she allowed herself to envision an alternative reality where she joined Adam on his nighttime runs. She shuffled back toward the living room, her mind reeling with thoughts of sweating gym clothes, after work-out showers and whatever Adam did all by himself in his big, empty home. As soon as Charlotte returned to the couch, all sordid thoughts of her neighbor, his fitness regime and what he looked like under those sweatpants came to a screeching halt. Her hand flew to her mouth as she stifled yet another gasp.

The library book was gone.

Chapter Seven

Chapter Seven

April 9, 1913

I continue to feel unwell. In fact, my symptoms seem to be intensifying. For the last week, my thoughts have been muddled and bolstered by dizzy spells. Of course, mother blames the heat and my restrictive garments, but I feel like this all the time. The patterns in the living room rug move. The walls speak to me. And when I am in Martin's presence, the feeling is worse than ever.

There is still no word from George, and I am beginning to suspect the worst. Mother assures me that he is just busy with his lectures, but I am doubtful. Martin tells me over tea while I am sitting for his portrait that I deserve better. I don't deserve anything. I'm the spoiled daughter of a cookie tycoon. There is no pity or concern from anyone for me.

I would write more, but I am tired now. Hopefully our trip to Tybee Island next week will renew me. In all honesty, I am most eager to leave Roser Park, even if it's for a short time.

Chapter Eight

Chapter Eight
"Yeah, the book just disappeared."

Charlotte pressed her sweaty ear to her phone the following morning as she leaned against the kitchen counter. The teakettle let out a low whistle and she poured herself a cup of instant coffee. Laurence basked in the early morning light of the back windows, oblivious and happy as always. On the other line she could hear her nieces and nephew screaming at each other while the television blared. Despite the noise, she ached for their familiar scent and the safety of her sister's home.

"Maybe you put it somewhere else and forgot? Dakota, cut it out!" Emma's voice was impatient and harried over the phone.

Charlotte knew that the morning probably wasn't the best time to call, but she needed to hear a friendly voice. "I hope so. This house is huge. I just don't want to have to pay the library back if I really lost it. That book probably cost a small fortune."

"Everything else okay?" Emma sighed. "You sound, I dunno... *tired*."

"I'm fine I guess." Charlotte lied. "I think I'm allergic to something in this house. I feel all out of whack sometimes, like I have vertigo or something."

"All of those old houses are probably chock full of mold. They look good on the outside, but the foundations are rotten. William, get off the table *now*!"

Charlotte winced and rose from her seat. Maybe going back to live with her sister wouldn't be the best plan of action at the moment after all. "I'll try some allergy meds and see if it helps. I think maybe my body is just finally crashing after the last year. I've forgotten how to relax."

"That's the truth." Emma chuckled. "What about the hot gardener guy?"

"What about him?" Charlotte smiled into the phone.

"Well, it's nice that you're interested in someone and all, but I just think you should be... careful."

"I *am* being careful." Charlotte rolled her eyes.

"Well, will you at least give me his full name so I can look the guy up? You can never be *too* careful these days."

"Mueller. Adam Mueller, of 682 Roser Park Drive."

"Mueller? Like the painting lady?" Emma's voice raised.

"Yeah, I guess she was a distant aunt." Charlotte said. "His family founded the neighborhood. I think Adam might secretly be rich."

"Well, I'll find out for sure." Emma muffled a kiss

through the phone. "Sorry, Char. I gotta get these kids to school. Call me later."

"Bye, Em." Charlotte tossed her phone on the counter, poured a cup of coffee, and took a long, thoughtful sip. She winced and stuck out her tongue. "Ew."

Laurence lifted his head and gazed up at her. He stretched, rose, and started circling, his little nails tapping away.

"I know. Time for a walk." Charlotte sighed and dumped the contents of her cup down the drain. "I could use a decent cup of coffee anyway."

Laurence yipped in appreciation as Charlotte grabbed his leash from the hook. She grimaced at the acrid taste in her mouth and reached for a bottle of water from the fridge. Cold H2O would have to do until she reached the little café almost a mile from the neighborhood.

"It's a long walk to the coffee shop, Larry." Charlotte latched the leash around the dog's collar. "Think you can handle it?"

The Yorkie spun in circles like a furry little bundle of nerves. Charlotte didn't know who was more anxious to get out of the house, her, or the dog. With her head still light and fuzzy, she determined that a long walk would do them both good. She secured the house and let an excited Laurence lead the way through the back door and out into the yard.

The day was clear and full of promise as she and the dog took off down the street. She snorted to herself as they trotted together along the brick-lined street like her own little Toto. She sucked in a deep breath and smiled as a young woman on a bike approached on the other side of the road. Charlotte had seen her during other walks, all long limbs and dark, glossy hair. They had exchanged pleasant smiles a few times before, but never exchanged words. This time, the girl brought the tires of her bike to a screeching halt.

"Hey." The girl glanced at the dog and then back at Charlotte again.

"Hey." Charlotte smiled. "Nice day."

"It is." The girl stared at Laurence again and pointed. "Does that dog live over there?"

Charlotte followed the trajectory of the girl's pointed finger back toward the Collier's house. "Yeah. I'm house-sitting and taking care of him. I'm Charlotte."

The girl nodded; her lips set in a sort of half frown. "Jasmine."

"Do you live here in the neighborhood?" Charlotte pursed her lips and raised a hand to her brow.

The girl couldn't have been older than, what, eighteen? Nineteen? It was hard to say.

"Sort of." The corners of her lips turned down.

"Do you know the Colliers?" Charlotte ventured.

"No." She huffed. "But I know that dog. My friend was hired to take care of him a couple of weeks ago."

"Oh great, maybe I know her. Is she still a student at the college?" Charlotte offered a hopeful smile. Even though the girl was likely half her age, it was still nice to have someone to talk to. Still, as she assessed her new acquaintance, it was obvious that the girl was uncomfortable.

"I don't think so." Jasmine's frown deepened. "We haven't heard from her in a while. She's missing."

"Oh. I'm sorry to hear that." Charlotte winced. "Wait, are you friends with Rochelle?"

The girl paused, and shifted in her bike seat, refusing to meet Charlotte's eye. "I gotta go."

Without uttering another word, Jasmine huffed and pedaled off down the road, her hair flying behind her.

"Hey, wait!" She waved and called after her, but she turned a corner and was gone. Charlotte gazed down at Laurence under heavy brows. He looked back at her with his tongue out. "Guess that's what I get for trying to be friendly."

With a shrug and a shake of her head, Charlotte popped in her earbuds and continued toward the café. Her body craved caffeine too much at that point to be bothered by the cryptic neighborhood teen on the bike. Maybe the last house-sitter did have a party and the girl had been there. Either way, the interaction left her more than a little unsettled.

Charlotte only half listened to her podcast as she continued down the road, passing dozens of multi-million-dollar homes, each as pristine and lushly landscaped as Judy and Garrett's house. It occurred to her that Adam likely cared for all these homes, each of them affecting the same finished look of perfectly pruned precision. Laurence stopped now and then to sniff a mailbox or something suspicious on the side-walk but managed to keep a surprisingly good pace for such an old dog. Ten and then fifteen minutes passed until they finally reached the little coffee shop situated outside of downtown St. Petersburg. Her heart sank a little as she reached the entryway and realized that Laurence may pose a problem.

"Hope this is a pet-friendly establishment." She scooped the little dog up in her arms. "Be quiet and look cute."

A welcomed wall of icy air and the scent of roasted coffee beans hit Charlotte as she crossed the threshold into the Roser Café. To her utter delight, the place was nearly empty, save for the lone barista behind the counter. Her eye was instantly drawn to a glass storage container of dog treats. She sighed and placed Laurence on the floor.

"Welcome." The person behind the counter greeted her with a smile, eyes bright behind a set of thick plastic frames. "What can I get for you?"

She sighed and leaned against the counter. "Just a black coffee, please. Large."

"You got it."

Charlotte reached for a dog treat but thought better of it. Laurence looked up at her, his tongue lolling to one side and his face sweet and full of anticipation. She didn't know what was in the treats and didn't want to interfere with his special diet.

"That's going to be $2.12." The barista slid the cup of coffee across the counter.

Charlotte handed over three singles. "Is this café open every day? I'm staying at a place down the street, and I can't get the coffee there to taste right."

"Mhmm." The barista nodded and handed her the change.

She dumped the change in the empty tip jar and added another dollar for good measure. "Well, I'll probably be seeing more of you then. Thanks again."

"Have a good day."

Charlotte took a deep sip of the piping hot beverage as she and Laurence headed out toward home. The coffee burned as it traveled down her throat, but instantly she could tell that the walk and the four dollars was well worth it. There would be no way that she could focus on her course work without a sweet dose of caffeine. By the time she and Laurence returned to the Collier's home, Charlotte's coffee cup was empty, and her spirits were raised. She had worn a proper pair of breathable walking shorts to battle her rubbing thighs. The sky was blue, the birds were singing. In the daytime the Roser Park neighborhood was quite lovely and walking alongside the creek made the trip almost peaceful.

Her idyllic morning was short-lived as the house in her charge came into view. There, pruning hedges and sweating profusely under the shade of a jacaranda tree was none other than Adam. Whether from the jolt of java or the prospect of speaking to the broody neighbor, Charlotte's pulse suddenly sped up.

"Hi." Charlotte waved as she approached.

Adam glanced up at her from under the brim of his cap. He tipped the bill as she approached. "Hey."

"Had to go up the street for some coffee." Charlotte raised her empty cup. "I can't seem to figure out how to make a good cup here."

"Oh." Adam dropped his shears into a nearby wheelbarrow and lowered his gaze. "You should just come over here next time. I always brew a full pot, but I never seem to finish it."

Charlotte's already hot cheeks flushed. "That's really generous. I don't want to impose."

"No imposition at all. Just come on over." Adam said. He glanced down at Laurence who was busy sniffing at the hedge that separated the two houses. "You both doing okay?"

"Fine, yeah. Thank you again for checking on me last night." Charlotte sucked in a deep, slow breath and smiled. "I'm not always this jumpy, I swear."

"Don't worry about it." His gaze flicked up at the side of the Collier's house and then back down to the ground again. "Must be strange staying at someone else's place."

"It's a little disorienting." She nodded. "House sitting has its benefits though. I finally get a little peace and quiet so I can study."

"Oh yeah? Are you in school or something?" Adam removed his baseball cap and scratched the back of his head, his gaze locking with hers again.

For a moment, Charlotte forgot what he even said. Whether from the surge of pure caffeine or the brisk walk, she felt awake again for the first time in days. Still, his slow, easy smile and warm, dark eyes were easy to get lost in. She blinked and shook her head. "Nursing! I'm going to school for nursing. Just started."

"Nice." He smiled and propped his hands on his hips. "I've been thinking of taking some business courses myself. Maybe try to expand and get a few employees eventually."

"That's a great idea." She nodded. "I felt a little insecure signing up at first. Everyone in most of my classes is young enough to be my kid."

"Hmm." Adam laughed and offered up another warm smile. "It's not too late for us yet."

"No." She shook her head. "I guess it's not."

Adam glanced over her shoulder and the soft, sweet expression that she had allowed herself to become so enthralled in, fell. Her eyes narrowed as she followed his gaze to the large white flowering tree at the side of the property. The one that Gary had expressly mentioned for her to never, never let Laurence near.

"Oh, no." Adam pushed past her into the yard and marched to the side of the house. He stopped just short of the flowering bush where a dozen or so white blossoms had dropped into the thick carpet of grass.

Charlotte muffled a scream. Laurence's leash, which had been taut and tugged at her the entire morning, had gone slack.

Adam scooped up a small, still bundle of fur from beneath the flowering bush and moved faster than she could react. He grabbed her arm and pulled her toward his work truck. Time slowed as she opened the door and slid into his passenger seat on autopilot.

"Here." Adam's eyes were dark and serious as he handed her the limp little dog. "We need to get him to an emergency vet. *Now.*"

Chapter Nine

Chapter Nine

"I'm a terrible dog sitter. The worst."

Charlotte cradled her head in her hands as she sat and waited in the Southside Emergency Vet Clinic later that morning. Adam waited silently at her side with his elbows resting on his knees and fingers steepled at his lips. Even though he raced them to the vet in record time, Charlotte couldn't help but worry. If Laurence died, she would never be able to forgive herself.

"I've told Judy and Garrett that it's irresponsible to keep that damned plant." Adam huffed. "It's over a hundred years old though. They don't wanna give it up."

"So, you think that's what it is?" Charlotte sniffed. "How could he have eaten one of the flowers? I only took my eyes off him for a minute."

"I don't know. The vet should probably be able to say. Either way, don't blame yourself. Someone was bound to get hurt eventually."

"What do you mean?" Charlotte sucked in a deep

breath and sat up. It had been a long time since she had sat in a veterinarian's waiting room. It wasn't unlike being in a hospital; underneath the animal smells there was still that same distinct scent of chemicals, sickness, and death.

"I mean, they should at least put up a gate around the bush or something." Adam glanced over at her; his features pinched. "I've had to chase off neighborhood teens more than once trying to get to the flowers."

"What do teenagers want with them?" Charlotte tore away from Adam's gaze and stared down at the high-shine terrazzo floor.

"What do teenagers always want? Trouble, that's what." Adam scoffed. "They use the flowers to get high. You can eat 'em or make a kind of tea with them. If you're not careful though, they're deadly."

"How are these plants even legal?" Charlotte crossed her arms at her chest and thought back to her run-in with the girl on the bike. "I wonder if that's why Jasmine was asking if I was staying in the house."

"Who?"

"Some girl that lives in the neighborhood. She was asking if I was staying at Judy and Garrett's house. Probably wanted to stake out the place."

"Exactly why I think they should get rid of it." Adam tugged the brim of his hat down.

"There's enough trouble out there for teenagers to get themselves wrapped up in. No sense in practically laying it out on a platter for them."

"Miss Slater?" A vet tech emerged through the back door and waved for her.

Charlotte rose from her seat on wobbly legs, her heart hammering away again. Her eyes flicked to Adam.

He offered a smile. "I'll wait here."

Charlotte nodded and followed the vet tech to the same dark back room where Laurence was whisked away twenty minutes before.

"He's going to be fine." The vet tech nodded. "Dr. Mathias had to pump his stomach, but you got him here just in time."

Charlotte's heart nearly broke as she approached the dog. His eyes were sleepy, but he wagged his tail for her.

"We'd like to keep him overnight for observation." The vet tech said. "We just have some forms for you to fill out at the front desk."

"Hey, buddy." Charlotte choked on her words as she scratched the dog's head. His eyes were closed but she could clearly see his pink belly rise and fall. She hadn't realized until that moment that she had already grown attached to the little guy.

"He's a lucky fella. Good thing he's got youth on his side." The vet tech smiled and scribbled on her clipboard.

"What do you mean?" She frowned. "He's a senior dog."

The vet tech shook her head. "He's only two. He was here just last month for his physical."

Charlotte's lower lip fell open. "I don't understand. His owners told me he was old and needed a special diet."

The vet tech shrugged. "I just know what's on the chart. Anyway, you can pick him up after seven a.m. tomorrow. We'll take good care of him until then."

"Okay." Charlotte sighed and gave Laurence one last pet for good measure. "See you in the morning, pal."

The vet tech led Charlotte away from the darkened room toward the front desk. She signed a stack of papers in a daze, grateful at least that Adam had taken her to the vet office where Judy and Garrett already had an account. Though she was grateful that Laurence would pull through, she re-entered the waiting room with even more questions than she began with.

"Hey." Adam greeted her with a crooked smile. "What's the word?"

"He's fine." Charlotte hugged herself. "They're keeping him overnight for observation."

"That's a relief." Adam rose from his seat and followed her out of the office into the parking lot. His keys jingled and swayed at his hips as they walked. She blinked at the sound. Suddenly Charlotte didn't feel quite so safe with him anymore. She glanced at him from the corner of her eye as he opened the passenger side door of his truck.

"How did you know that this was the vet that Judy and Garrett used?"

Adam frowned and looked up at the building, then back at her. "I didn't. This was just the closest place."

"Oh." She paused for another moment. Her body was telling her to run. Her head told her she was being silly. Paranoid. Bile rose in her throat. She pursed her lips and swallowed it down. "They told me that Laurence isn't as old as I thought he was."

Adam shifted and scratched the bridge of his nose. "How old did you think he was?"

"I don't know exactly. I thought he was a geriatric dog with medical issues. It's the whole reason the Collier's hired me."

Adam shook his head. "I don't think they've even had this dog for more than a couple of years. They've always had little Yorkie dogs for as long as I've known them, but Laurence is fairly new."

Charlotte sucked in a shuddered breath. "Something is weird. I need to call Judy and Garrett."

"Let me get you back home then." Adam opened his truck door wider. "Hop in."

Charlotte reluctantly climbed in. He shut the door behind her as she tried to remember how far they drove to get to the vet. Everything happened in a blur that morning and she had cried most of the way, clutching Laurence and paying no attention to the road. Walking back to the house probably wasn't an option, but she couldn't ignore the pit of uncertainty in her stomach either. She glanced back at Adam as he slid behind the wheel and shot her a wide smile. Why did he always happen to be around when she needed help?

She dug her hand down into her pocket and gripped

her house keys as he slid his keys into the ignition, his truck rumbling to life. Despite every bone in her body telling her not to trust him, she stayed. She had daylight on her side, and the veterinarian's office had cameras all around. She reasoned that if he wanted to do something bad, he would have had plenty of other opportunities to do it by now. Still, as they headed back toward the Roser Park neighborhood in silence, she kept as far to the right side of the truck as possible and prayed she wouldn't have to use the house keys as brass knuckles.

After what seemed like only a few moments of driving, the Roser Park neighborhood came back into view. Adam remained quiet behind the wheel as they drove, allowing her to examine the interior of his truck and take stock of her surroundings. For a work vehicle, the seats, carpet, and console were relatively spotless. There wasn't a lick of garbage or a foul smell at all in the modest truck cab, only the scent of a hanging pine air freshener and the sound of classic rock floating softly from the speakers.

As 684 Roser Park Drive drew near, Charlotte was finally able to relax a little. There was something alarming about him that she couldn't put her finger on, something familiar. Still, she was going to have to share a property line with him for the time being. An icebreaker was in order. "So, you probably take care of all of these lawns, huh?"

Adam glanced over at her from behind the wheel.

"Yeah, almost every house. It's not easy to find a landscaper in this area that will tackle the big hills."

"Why do you do it?" Charlotte stared out the window. "I mean, what made you decide on landscaping for a career?"

He cleared his throat and shrugged. "It just kind of fell in my lap I guess. It's good money, and it keeps me busy. Plus, I like being outside."

"You do a great job." She still couldn't fully relax. Adam pulled his truck into the driveway under an umbrella of overhanging leaves. The cool shade from the dense branches was a welcome reprieve.

"Thanks." He threw the truck into park and cut the engine. "Landscaping isn't really what I want to do, but it's satisfying enough."

"What is it that you want to do then?" Charlotte scanned his expression, her gaze falling to his lips. She sucked in a quick, sharp breath and blinked.

Adam eased into his seat but kept his hands clenched on the wheel. "I was a musician. I actually had a little success right out of high school. Didn't work out though."

"Oh yeah? What did you play?" Charlotte stared out the window toward the looming old house. It was going to feel even emptier than usual without Laurence around.

"Guitar. Acoustic, mostly."

"Do you still play for fun at least?"

Adam shook his head. "I try, but I have a hard time sitting still these days."

"It's okay. I don't do a lot of things I used to either." Charlotte sighed, more eager than ever to end their small talk. "Well, I guess I better get going. Thank you for helping today."

"I really am sorry about Laurence." Adam offered up a crinkle-eyed frown. "I hope that Judy and Garrett will listen to reason now after this happened at least."

"We can only hope." Charlotte opened the passenger side door and stepped down from Adam's truck. Her eyes flicked up to the second-floor picture window that overlooked both his yard and the Collier's yard. From her view in his driveway, she had a clear shot of the second-floor landing. Her gaze fixed on the very spot where Adam had locked eyes with her not long ago; the spot outside of the upstairs bedroom that felt exposed and off-center. Her eyes adjusted to the glare reflecting from the panes of glass when a flash of something black moved. All the air sucked from her lungs. She gasped and clamped her hand over her mouth.

"What? What is it?" Adam followed her gaze and scratched his jawline.

Charlotte licked her lips, and opened her mouth, her voice just above a whisper. "I think someone is in the house."

Chapter Ten

Chapter Ten

April 30,1913

The trip to Tybee Island did my head and heart a world of good. Savannah really was a lovely town, but I think being away from Roser Park in general lifted my spirits. Perhaps I can encourage George to move his practice there once we are married. The squares, parks and waterfront are quite charming though many people claim the town to be haunted as well. Ghosts are everywhere I suppose.

Mother caught wind of my plan to visit the psychic downtown. She's bringing Father Michael here this weekend instead to talk some sense into me. I think that she's been reading my entries here, Dear Diary. I'll have to find a new hiding spot for you.

Martin is nearly finished with my portrait, or so he says. I don't care to ever see the blasted thing or him ever again. I can't imagine that my expression is all that pleasant, I was in such pain and distress for all my sittings. I can't help but feel that this house, or rather something in it, is to blame.

I haven't seen the woman in the window since I've been home. Perhaps that's a good thing. If I should see her again, I won't let myself be frozen in fright. This time I swear I'll communicate with her once and for all.

Chapter Eleven

Chapter Eleven

"It's all clear in there, Miss."

"It's Ms., actually." Charlotte hugged her arms to her chest as two St. Petersburg Police officers emerged from inside Judy and Garrett's home.

"Huh?" The tall, slender cop with an ironic mustache looked at her sideways.

"Nevermind." She frowned back at them; her features pinched into what she was certain was not a pretty expression. At that moment, she didn't give a damn about how she looked. "So, you really didn't find anything?"

The younger officer shook her head and flipped open her notebook. "No, m'am. Now, you say the homeowners are out of town?"

"Yes. I'm just the house sitter." She shuddered despite the warm weather. "The owners — Mr. and Mrs. Collier — they're on a cruise in the Mediterranean."

The senior officer nodded. "We'll try to give them a call at the number you gave us then."

"So, really? There was no sign of forced entry

or anything out of place?" Charlotte hugged herself tighter. She knew that she had seen *something*. Either someone was in the house, or she would have something new and worrisome to discuss with her therapist.

"No. The alarm was set just like you said. Everything in there looked ship-shaped." The younger officer exchanged a glance with her partner. "Is there anyone else you would like us to call for you?"

Charlotte shook her head. "No. I'll be fine. Thank you again for coming out."

"We'll be in touch, then." The senior officer tipped his hat as they retreated toward their squad cars. "Take care now."

She gazed over at Adam as the police pulled out of the drive. He was still leaned up against his truck where he had been waiting the entire time while Charlotte filled out the report. Once again, Adam managed to jump to action on her behalf and called the police out before she could even think to dial 9-1-1.

"Well, that's two times today that you've had to witness me fall apart." Charlotte sniffed and shuffled toward his truck. "I suppose you must think I'm some kind of basket case."

Adam smirked and shook his head. "It's been a heck of a day."

"Judy and Garrett aren't going to pay me after all this." Charlotte pressed her fingertips to her swollen eyes. She hadn't cried this much in months.

"I suppose you should call them." Adam shrugged. "At least try to get to them before the cops do."

"Good point." Charlotte slipped her phone from her back pocket and scrolled through her contacts and dialed the number Judy had given her. The phone went straight to voicemail with Judy's chirpy voice instructing to leave a message.

"Hey . . . Judy. It's Charlotte. Could you and Garrett please call me when you get a chance? Thanks."

Charlotte killed the call and slid the phone back into her pocket. She shuddered despite the warm weather and gazed back up at the house. "I don't know if I can go back in there."

"Want me to come in with you?" Adam stood up straight and offered a shy grin. "I mean, I can go and scope it out with you, if it will make you feel better."

A corset of anxiety squeezed at her chest. House sitting was supposed to be relaxing. Easy money. She didn't know if she could stand staying in the house much longer, but she couldn't exactly walk away from it either. Plus, there was still Laurence to think about. She had to dig in her heels and finish what she started.

Charlotte shook her head. "You've already done so much. I don't want to take up any more of your time."

"I wouldn't offer if I didn't have time." Adam shoved his hands deep in his pockets.

Charlotte turned toward the house and flexed the hand that had been gripping her keychain. The teeth from the house keys left tiny triangular impressions in the palm of her hand. "I suppose a little company wouldn't hurt."

Adam's heavy footsteps fell behind her as they ascended the wraparound porch and Charlotte's heart dropped into her stomach as she approached the door. She sucked in another ragged breath and gazed over at him; a stranger, albeit a ridiculously handsome one. She didn't even like being vulnerable around people she knew well. At this point, she didn't have much of a choice.

"This isn't the only strange thing that has happened since I got here." Charlotte wrapped her hand around the doorknob. "I just wanted you to know. I'm not an irrational person. Weird things just keep happening."

Adam's expression didn't move or flinch. "Like what?"

Charlotte opened the door into the darkened hallway. The silence that filled the house was almost too loud. Heartbreaking even. There was no little tapping of nails on the hardwood floor to greet her. It would be only her and the house and her overactive imagination for the night. The thought filled her with dread.

"Well, like last night. When you heard me scream? I was startled because a library book fell on the floor when I was in the kitchen. I was sure I had placed it on the sofa."

"The house is probably on a slant." Adam shrugged. "I know mine is. Maybe the book just slid off?"

"That's what I thought at first too." Charlotte

ventured into the living room. "But then after you left, the book was completely gone."

"Like, disappeared?"

"Yeah. There's no way I could have misplaced . . . it." Charlotte halted dead in her tracks. There, on the couch, as if it was waiting for her, was the library book.

"Is that the one?" Adam shuffled over to the couch and picked up the heavy book. "History of Roser Park?"

"See! This is what I'm talking about. This place is messing with me." Charlotte reached for the book. "That's not all though. I keep hearing things. My laptop got busted. My drinking glasses keep getting moved. And I think I keep seeing someone."

Adam smirked and handed over the book. "Maybe the house is haunted."

"I wish." Charlotte snorted. "Ghosts I can handle. It's people that terrify me."

"Good point." Adam stood with his hands on his hips and surveyed the room.

Charlotte clutched the book to her chest, half grateful that it wasn't lost, and half creeped out that it returned.

"Want me to go check upstairs?" Adam knitted his brow together and glanced at the staircase.

"You don't have to." Charlotte placed the book down on the side table. "I'm just being paranoid. I'll be fine."

Adam scratched his head and gazed back at her

with his impossible brown eyes. "Do you have a way to pick up the dog from the vet tomorrow?"

Charlotte paused. She hadn't really considered how she would get Laurence home. "No. I suppose I can just call a car service though."

"Well, if you need a ride, you know where to find me." He nodded, his usually soft expression now somewhat withdrawn.

Charlotte was utterly exhausted and should have been relieved that he was leaving, but still felt unsettled about everything. Maybe she was misjudging Adam after all. She followed him on still shaky legs to the front door and considered bolting, running out the front door and down Roser Park Drive and never returning. The thought of the adorable above garage studio apartment that would be available next month stayed at the forefront of her mind, the one within walking distance from the college and the hospital. The apartment she could only afford if she finished this one last gig. Perhaps she could hold on for just a little longer.

"Thank you again. I'll let you know when Laurence is home safe."

Adam turned to her as he crossed the threshold into the waning afternoon light. He closed his eyes and nodded. "Take care of yourself."

"I will." She closed the door behind him before she could say or do something she would regret.

Chapter Twelve

Chapter Twelve

Sleep was next to impossible for Charlotte that night. With no way to complete her coursework and no dog to keep her company, she was left with her thoughts and the echoing walls of 684 Roser Park. She called her sister but was sent straight to voicemail. Emma was busy with her own family and her own life, and she felt bad relying so heavily on her little sister. After everything she went through last year, family was all Charlotte had left.

Charlotte painted her nails, did a gentle yoga routine, and made herself dinner, but nothing seemed to effectively pass the time. She was anxious and bored but determined to resist the urge to knock on Adam's door. There was still a big part of her that distrusted him, even if he had only proved to be helpful and nice. Even if he listened to and believed every wild thing that came out of her mouth, safety and self-preservation were more important than falling back into old patterns or a new stranger's bed. She had used her marriage as a security blanket for far too long and was determined not to get lost now in some misguided infatuation. She had failed to trust her gut in the past and where did it get her? Nowhere good. No. She wouldn't repeat that mistake again.

The giant leatherbound library book stared up at her from the living room side table as she scrolled through her phone, trying to numb out. Her eyes flicked up to the painting of Mary Mueller, her sad, somber expression forever staring down at her. At this point, Charlotte didn't care to know any more about the historic house and neighborhood. She was done with Roser Park and all its so-called history and mystery. But she did want to know about Mary Mueller. Perhaps there would be something about her sad painted companion in the book after all.

Charlotte tossed her phone on the couch cushions and grabbed the library book, flipping to the section of the book where she remembered seeing Mary's portrait. The first few chapters were about her family — the Mueller's — who lived in the property next door and founded the neighborhood. Her father, Horace, had invented a process for mass packaging cookies that had brought the family enough fortune to found their own upscale Florida subdivision. Her mother, Eugenia, was a socialite who dabbled in fundraising and charity work. There were two other children besides Mary: Samuel and Charles, no doubt one of Adam's great-grandfathers. There was a brief mention of Mary's passing in 1913 at the age of twenty-two, though no official cause of death was listed. The mother, Eugenia also passed that same year from "misfortune" due to a carriage accident.

Frustrated, Charlotte leafed through the book, finally landing on a page showing the Greenwood Cemetery. It was the final resting place of the Roser Park elite, and no doubt would be where she could find Mary Mueller's grave. The address showed that it was only a few blocks away and Charlotte made a mental note to walk that way on her next jaunt with Laurence.

Laurence.

Her heart ached and she cringed thinking about what she would tell Judy and Garret when they finally called back. *If* they finally called back. She thought again about Adam's offer to drive her to the vet in the morning. Maybe it wasn't such a bad idea after all.

Just as she was about to reach for her phone, the couch began to vibrate. Her phone was on silent, and she knew that it must have been lost once again in the depths of the overstuffed velvet couch. Like before, Charlotte plunged her hand into the depths of the cushions in search of her phone and her hand closed around a smooth, rectangular object. Only this time, her nail made direct contact with something sharp.

"Ah!" Charlotte winced and pulled her hand from the couch cushions in pain. A smatter of blood trickled from beneath the nail bed of her freshly manicured middle finger.

"Great." She moaned and stuck her finger in her mouth on instinct. She sucked at the metallic taste of herself and grimaced. "Perfect. Now I'm probably going to get tetanus."

Charlotte glanced down at the couch cushion and her attention was instantly moved from her throbbing, injured finger to the curious pink phone on the couch. She frowned and picked up the flip phone, which clearly did not belong to her. The device was old and dead, its painted edges worn, and the back side covered in faded stickers and press-on jewels.

"What in the?" She turned the phone over in her hand and stared back at the couch cushions again. Carefully, she eased her other hand into the couch, found her own phone and glanced at the screen. A missed call from Emma. She sighed and stared down at the almost vintage pink mystery phone in her hand. Perhaps it was left by one of the teenagers at some party another house sitter threw? Either way, she didn't have the proper adapter to plug it in and see who it belonged to.

THUD.

Charlotte's gaze flew to the ceiling. All thoughts of mystery phones and injured fingers were forgotten as her pulse quickened. From what she could gather, the distinct but faint sound of something falling had come from the locked rooms upstairs.

Charlotte.

The same disembodied voice from the library called to her again. Her heart picked up pace, beating so wildly now that she could hear the blood rush in her ears. The sickly-sweet scent of rotten flowers returned, and the soft swish of heavy fabric drifted up the stairs. Charlotte fought against her fears and turned her head just in time to see the hem of a long black skirt disappear toward the second floor.

She stood on shaky legs and eyed the front door. She could just leave. Laurence would be fine at the veterinarian. The house would be fine all on its own. The money didn't matter anymore.

Charlotte.

Her gaze flicked to the portrait of Mary Mueller again. Charlotte didn't believe in ghosts, but she did believe in herself. She wasn't an unreasonable person. She didn't normally see or hear things. But maybe Mary was trying to show her something.

Charlotte.

She knew if she left Roser Park and all of this behind, she might never find out. Besides, if the voice was at the library, who's to say it wouldn't follow her to her sister's home? The last thing she wanted was to terrorize her nieces and nephew. No. She couldn't run. *Something* was calling to her. Charlotte sucked in a shaky breath and headed toward the stairs against every shred of good sense she ever had.

The first step was the hardest. However, with every move, Charlotte felt more and more emboldened. Something pulled her back up the stairs to a part of the home she had no interest in ever returning to. Everything in her being told her to turn around and forget all of this. She had failed to listen to her instincts so many times before. This time was different though.

As she neared the landing, it was clear that the door to the small bedroom on the left was halfway open. An obtuse triangle of light spilled out into the darkened upstairs hall, even though she knew that she had closed that door and never even turned on a lamp. The doors of the other upstairs room were all still shut tight, and the closer she got to the eerie little room, the more intense the decayed floral fragrance became. She steeled herself and peered into the room.

Charlotte was half-expecting to be greeted by the skeleton of Mary Mueller perched on the bed, sitting primly in a black taffeta mourning gown, her rivulets of strawberry blonde hair caressing ivory cheekbones. Thankfully, the room was empty and just as she had left it a few days before. Instead of some specter or intruder, though, Charlotte saw something else. Her eyes were drawn to the floor at the foot of the bed where something had been left for her to find. Something very old and small in the shape of a book.

Pick it up.

A cold thrill shivered down her spine. Working on pure adrenaline, Charlotte grabbed the small, leather-bound book, turned, and bolted down the stairs away from the musty, floral scent of death and whatever else lurked on the second floor.

Chapter Thirteen

Chapter Thirteen

May 1st, 1913

Mother has died. I am heartbroken, weak, and barely able to write to you, Dear Diary. I am in such poor condition that I couldn't even attend her funeral, though father said I wouldn't have wanted to. After the horse trampled her, an open casket was not possible. The damage a hoof must do to one's face. Even though I was not there to witness it, her poor crumpled body is all I can see.

Martin has come to visit me every day since to bring me tea and snacks. He says that he is still working on the portrait, though my father has forgotten all about it in his sorrow. I hope that I never see the damned thing.

George still has not written, and there is no word from his family. It is almost as though I no longer exist to them or anyone else. My friends no longer come to call. I am too weak to take part in my pastimes. My family is withdrawn into themselves, lost in their own grief.

I've tried everything to get my father to have a real physician to come see me. I am ashamed to admit that I have even taken to eating strange things to evoke some sort of emotion in him. First it was chunks of goose feather from my pillow. Next, I tore a strip of wallpaper from behind my bed, rolled it up and ate it just like a Parisian crepe. I even took a bite out of mothers' favorite china teacup. I think the sight of my mouth dripping with blood might have finally stirred a reaction in him. Father threatened to send me to the psychiatric hospital in Jacksonville, and I was almost overjoyed until Martin stepped in. He insisted that I move in with him and his wife next door instead. The good doctor. He says that his wife can help to nurse me and care for me since my mother is gone.

Dear Diary, I don't know if I will survive if I am left solely in Martin's care. I feel it in my bones that this house — that Martin — is the reason I am losing my grip on reality. George, if you should ever read this, please know that I am sorry. I wish I could be stronger. I wish —

Chapter Fourteen

Chapter Fourteen
Charlotte closed the diary of Mary Mueller, her pulse hammering wildly in her chest. She was *right*. Mary *had* been trying to tell her something. She flipped back toward the beginning of the diary which was dated in early 1912 when the family moved into the house. The first few pages dripped with the happy thoughts of a young woman, hopeful and exuberant about life. Mary listed her daily activities, outings with her friends, her hopes for the future with her fiancé, all in an elegant, perfectly finished hand. Her tone became markedly different in early 1913, and the name Martin began to appear on every page. Towards the end, her penmanship was little more than a scrawl.

BANG, BANG, BANG.

Charlotte gasped and glanced up at the front door. She had become so engrossed with reading Mary's journal that she lost track of the time. A quick check of her phone showed seven missed calls from her sister. It was nearly eleven at night.

"Char? Are you in there?" Emma's muffled voice sounded from the other side of the door.

"One sec!" Charlotte exhaled and rose from the couch. Still clutching the journal, she opened the front door to her very red-faced, very pissed-off looking sister.

"Oh my god, I thought you were dead." Emma pushed her way through the front door, her eyes darting back and forth. "Are you alone?"

"Yeah? What . . . why?" Charlotte closed the front door and locked the deadbolt. Her normally calm and collected sister frightened her more than the possibility of facing a ghost.

"I tried to call you a million times." Emma panted. "Your boyfriend Adam? Did he tell you that he was in prison?"

All the feeling left Charlotte's legs. "No."

"Well, that's not a surprise. I wouldn't advertise it either." Emma scoffed. "Five years is a long time."

"Wait. Let me think for a minute." Charlotte sunk back into the couch and massaged her temples, trying hard to not jump to conclusions. If she knew one thing, it was that it was unfair to judge someone without all the facts. "What was the crime?"

"Embezzlement. His family used to be rich." Emma moved to the front window and peered through the heavy curtains. She closed them and turned back to Charlotte. "Does this place have video surveillance?"

"I don't think so. They have a security system, but

I don't think they have cameras. Really, Em, what's wrong?"

Emma sighed and crossed her arms at her chest. "I don't think it's safe for you to be here anymore."

Charlotte rolled her eyes. "Not this again..."

"Please. Just trust your gut for once. These people are weird. They lied about the dog. Their neighbor is shady. Come on, Brad and I will loan you the money . . ."

"Stop." Charlotte chewed on her lower lip and paused a moment before speaking again. "I appreciate you trying to help, but I don't need your money. I have to try and figure this out myself."

"Fine, don't take the money. But really, listen to your gut. Something isn't right here."

Charlotte glanced up from the floor at her sister. She knew Emma was right. From the moment she set foot inside of the Roser Park house, something had felt off. She sensed it in her bones. She was tired of being the screwed up relative. Tired of having her little sister swoop in and save her. For once, Charlotte wanted to finish something and take care of it herself. And despite all the red flags, all the uneasy feelings, she still wanted to know why Mary Mueller was reaching out to her.

"I need to finish this, Em. I just want to see something through for once. Also, I need to show you something." Charlotte held up the diary.

Emma dropped her arms to her side. "What's that?"

"I found it upstairs." Charlotte glanced up at the

portrait on the wall. "It belonged to Mary Mueller. I keep hearing and seeing things. Smelling weird things. I think she's trying to tell me something."

Emma pursed her lips into a frown, brows knitted together as she took the diary. She flipped through the pages, her expression softening as she read the entries of the tortured woman.

"Em, you know I don't usually believe in ghosts. I'm not losing it, I promise."

Emma let out a deep sigh and made a face. A silent, heavy moment passed between the sisters. For once, the house, usually alive with sound, was silent and still. Her sister offered a half-smile, half-frown. "So, you're freaked out because you found the diary of this lady in the painting?"

"*Yes*. Don't you get it? This wasn't even her house! Why would her old diary just show up out of no-where?"

"I don't know." Emma grumbled under her breath and handed the book back. "I mean, why is her por-trait here for that matter? Who knows what the old owners traded back and forth over the years?"

Charlotte pushed out an exasperated sigh. "Em. The book wasn't there before. It just *appeared*."

"So, it's a ghost that likes old books then?" Emma raised her eyebrows and chuckled softly.

Charlotte's heart fell. Even her own sister didn't believe her.

"Listen, please take what I had to say at heart. It's not ghosts I'm worried about."

Charlotte rose from the couch and wrapped her sister in a reassuring hug. "I know."

Emma wiped at her eyes and turned back toward the door. "Just, please look out for yourself, okay?"

"I will." Charlotte held the door and watched her sister descend the stairs.

Emma turned halfway down and looked back up; her face drawn in the pale moonlight. "You can come home any time. I mean it."

Charlotte nodded. "I'll remember."

Emma hesitated as though she had something else to say, then turned again toward the road. Charlotte watched as her sister slipped behind the wheel of her minivan and waited for her to turn over the engine before closing the door.

Prison.

Emma's warning about Adam came from a place of concern and wasn't entirely unwarranted. Charlotte barely knew him as it was, and to be fair, being incarcerated was something she probably wouldn't disclose right away to someone she just met either. Perhaps her knee-jerk reaction to not trust the ever-smiling, helpful and handsome neighbor next door wasn't so irrational after all.

Charlotte armed the alarm system and yawned, finally feeling drowsy for the first time that evening. She tried to call Judy and Garrett at the number they provided again, but like before, the line rang and went to voicemail. The house remained quiet, the usual creaks and groans beneath the floor were still, as though the structure was holding its breath. Maybe her ghost was satisfied for the moment.

Still on edge, Charlotte fixed herself a cup of tea and headed back to her nest in the front room. It would have been so easy to walk away that night, slip into the safety of her sister's minivan, back to the familiar smells and sounds of home. It would be so easy to just give up and admit that she couldn't handle this simple house-sitting job. She was tired of taking the easy way out; tired of the pitiful looks her sister and everyone else gave her. For once, Charlotte Slater was going to see something through. With the found diary in her lap, and a million questions on her mind, she finally drifted off that night as Mary Mueller stood guard from her perch over the fireplace mantle with her ever watching eyes.

***

"That's going to be $875.00."

Charlotte blinked at the invoice in front of her as Laurence sat patiently in his carrier. It was 8 a.m. the following morning and a rideshare driver was waiting for her outside the veterinarian's office. She could scarcely afford the twenty bucks for the ride; almost nine hundred bucks was completely out of the question.

"Can't you charge this to the Collier's account?" She glanced up at the receptionist behind the desk and gave a weary smile. The woman pushed her frames up the bridge of her nose and shook her head.

"No, we don't really do that." The receptionist

pointed to a sign above her desk. "Payment due at time of service."

Charlotte reluctantly pulled out her credit card and handed it over. She rubbed her temples and bit her lower lip as the receptionist ran her card, her heart working overtime. She half expected the transaction to decline, and then what would happen? Her eyebrows raised as the woman stapled her receipt to the invoice and returned her card with a smile.

"You're all set. Dr. Mathias wants to see Laurence back in one week."

"Oh. Okay. Great." She blinked and folded the receipt and placed it in her bag. Judy and Garrett would have to refund her for the vet bill, right? She glanced down at her new furry friend and sighed. "Let's get you home then."

The entire ride home, Charlotte clutched the dog carrier in her lap from the backseat of the cab. She had practically blacked out the night before, whether from exhaustion or nerves, and was still feeling groggy and disoriented. Charging nearly a thousand dollars to her credit card for a dog that didn't even belong to her didn't help her mental and emotional state at that moment either. She needed to clear her head somehow and think.

Adam's truck and work trailer was gone from the driveway when she arrived back at the house. Her body relaxed at the realization that she wouldn't have to face him right away. She paid her tab, and as the driver pulled away, her eyes rested on the Datura bush. The whole reason for Laurence's vet stay. That and her carelessness. She had to admit that it was a pretty plant, with white angel trumpet floral bells that swayed softly amongst thick, green leaves. The day before, a bed of spent flower buds had littered the yard at the base of the plant. It occurred to her that Adam must have cleaned up the dangerous blossoms ahead of Laurence coming home.

The house was quiet and still as she entered the front room, taking careful, cautious steps. Laurence was tamer than usual and headed straight for his bed on the floor near the fireplace. She tried to call Judy and Garrett yet again, but still couldn't reach them. Her laptop wasn't due back for a few more days, and she didn't feel right leaving Laurence to go to the library just yet. Charlotte needed to admit defeat.

"What do you think about making it a pool day?" She sighed and cast her eyes toward the back yard. "Come on. Some fresh air will do us both good."

Laurence answered with a sigh.

"You know, for a furry creature with no responsibilities, you sure sigh a lot." Charlotte ruffled the top of his head, grabbed her swimsuit from her duffle and headed toward the bathroom, surprised to hear the gentle tapping of nails following her down the hall. She smiled as the dog followed her into the bathroom.

"Alright you little stalker." She smiled, bending down to pet him. "I could use a little privacy."

Before she could nudge him out the door, Laurence made a beeline past the claw foot tub toward the corner closet. She frowned, her head cocked to the side as she watched him sniff at the crack in the door, his tail wagging wildly.

"Oh, I see." Laurence let out a low growl, his nose trained toward the door. "That's where they have your treats hidden, huh?"

In a way, Charlotte was relieved to see him full of life again. She let him stay sniffing away at the door as she changed into her swimsuit.

"Okay, that's enough." She bent down to pick him up, her eyes trained on the strange closet door lock. Her hand shot out to touch it again, to try and turn the mismatched knob. Laurence growled in her arms, and a cold, sick sensation filled her gut. The scent of flowers. Mary was back.

"Let's go." She turned on shaky legs and grabbed a towel from the rack, once again making certain to avoid the mirror on her way out. If the ghost of Mary Mueller really was in the room with her, she wasn't prepared to face her. She sped past the kitchen with Laurence under her arm until she was finally safe out in the bright early morning light.

The pool was laid out and waiting for her; gorgeous, inviting, cerulean. Even though it was early in the day, the temperature was nearly ninety degrees. A dip in the pool was exactly what she needed. Her chest was still tight as she flicked her phone and found the music app. She placed Laurence on a nearby shaded recliner and secured his leash to the chair, hoping he would be comfortable enough for her to try and relax a little.

When she was certain the dog was settled, Charlotte stepped into the water, surprised to find that the pool was much colder than she anticipated. Still, the cool water was a relief, and she easily slid beneath the surface, letting the chlorinated water envelop her completely. There, under the shimmering blue, she could finally have real silence, a real moment to think clearly. She had done a lot of her best thinking that way as a child, flipping around and around under the water in her grandparents' pool. She didn't know how easy she had it back then.

Charlotte came to the surface gulping in air. A quick check told her that Laurence was happily resting, his eyes closed, and head tucked on top of his paws. She laid back in the pool and allowed her body to rise and be supported by hundreds of gallons of water. She floated there and stared up at the sky, cloudless save for a few stray puffs of cottony cumulous.

You're being irrational, Charlotte.

The words of her former husband wiggled into her brain, even as she tried to clear her mind.

You're just trying to find a problem where there isn't one.

She snorted. Well, maybe she *was* irrational. Or maybe a hundred-year-old ghost was trying to tell her something. She breathed in deeply, trying hard to put all her worries out of her mind. School. Money. Life.

All of it would get sorted in time. She just needed to be clear-headed long enough to think.

Just as her shoulders finally relaxed, a shadow blocked out the sun behind her closed eyelids. The sick feeling entered her gut again, and Charlotte knew that she wasn't alone.

Chapter Fifteen

Chapter Fifteen

Charlotte gasped and flailed, splashing as she struggled to right herself. A shadowy figure in the shape of a man hovered near the edge of the pool, unmoving. She clutched her hands to her chest and aspirated droplets of chlorinated water, choking as she tried to suck oxygen back into her lungs. Her pulse quickened as she backed toward the stairs.

"I'm sorry, I didn't mean to sneak up on you." Adam held up his hands in a gesture of apology.

With one last water choked cough, Charlotte nodded up and down, wiping at her eyes. "You scared the life out of me."

"Are you okay? Let me get you a towel." Adam moved to the chaise lounge where Laurence sat wagging his tail. He picked up the bathroom towel and handed it to her. Charlotte took it gratefully, hoping it was big enough to give her some level of modesty.

"It's fine. Thank you." Charlotte stepped out of the pool and covered herself in the towel. Normally she might have been self-conscious about being seen in her bathing suit by an attractive man, but at that moment, she only felt uneasy.

"I just wanted to come by and check on Laurence. And you."

She faked a smile. "We're doing fine. I think Laurence is much better. I saw that you cleaned up the blossoms that had dropped from the plant. Thank you."

"It's my job." He readjusted the brim of his baseball hat, his eyes trailing up and down her figure. "I was actually going to see if you had plans for dinner tonight."

Charlotte blinked. "Tonight? Oh, tonight I . . ."

"*Char-lotte*! Char! Are you back there?"

A wave of relief flooded through her chest. Emma. Saving the day. *Again.*

"I'm back here, Em!" Charlotte called out; her legs flooded with adrenaline . . .

Adam turned toward the sound of her sister's voice and then met her gaze again. "You expecting company?"

Charlotte shrugged. "Yeah, my sister. Sorry, we have plans tonight."

"Oh." He sighed and nodded. "Rain check then?"

Before she had a chance to answer, Emma rounded the corner dressed in her usual weekend uniform of sneakers, fitness tights and an oversized tee. At that moment, Charlotte had never been so grateful to see her.

"I knocked on the door. You need to answer your

phone," Emma scolded. She looked up and did a double-take at Adam. "Sorry. Am I interrupting something?"

"This is Adam, he's a neighbor. He just came to check on Laurence." She opened her eyes wide, hoping Emma would read her sisterly telepathy. "I forgot you were coming over to help me with my coursework. Adam, this is my sister, Emma."

Emma's eyes narrowed as she looked Adam up and down. She didn't bother to mask her distaste for him. "Right. Study time."

"Nice to meet you, Emma." Adam pulled his mega-watt smile. "Well, I won't intrude any further. You ladies have a good day."

"You too." Emma waved and threw him a look of pure disgust as he retreated from the edge of the pool.

Charlotte held her breath until he moved through the hedges and disappeared into his own backyard. When she was certain he was gone, she finally exhaled.

"I think you might have carved a hole in his back with that death glare." Charlotte finally greeted her sister with a wet hug. "What are you doing here? Doesn't Lacy have a soccer game?"

"Yeah, Brad has the kids today. I needed to come show you something."

"What is it? A listing for a non-profit mental health program?" Charlotte snorted. Still slightly shaken and dripping, she scooped Laurence up from the chair.

"Don't joke about that sort of thing." Emma

frowned. "I'm sorry for not believing you. I did some more digging."

"Oh yeah, what did you find? Another murder podcast? A haunted history of St. Petersburg featuring the ghost of Roser Park?"

"I'm serious." Emma scratched between the dog's ears. "How is he, anyway?"

"He seems to be okay. Cost me a small fortune though."

"What?"

Charlotte sighed and walked toward the house with Laurence under one arm. "I couldn't get hold of the owners and they wouldn't let me have him until I paid the bill."

Emma followed her inside, huffing. "I'm beginning to really dislike these people. They're in Europe, not outer space."

"I know. I didn't know what else to do, so I charged the vet bill on my card."

"Screw these people! Seriously, Char, just come back home with me. You can bring the dog."

"I can't. If I don't stay here at the house, then they definitely won't pay me." Charlotte gently lowered the dog to the floor. He padded over to his bowl and began to eat. "That's the other thing. He isn't really a special needs dog."

"What do you mean?"

"I mean the vet told me that he was perfectly healthy and only like two-years-old." Charlotte bit her thumbnail, her gaze trained on the little dog. "I just don't understand any of this."

"Okay, well if I can't convince you to get out of here, and a ghost can't convince you, then maybe Rochelle Davis can." Emma dug into the side pocket of her fitness tights and pulled out her phone. She began to scroll through a social media feed that Charlotte didn't recognize. Emma held out the phone for her to read.

"What's that?"

"It was the last post that Rochelle made before she went missing. Saying that she was going to a job interview."

Charlotte glanced at the message board emblazoned with emojis, exclamation points and wishes of good luck. Rochelle's smiling cartoon avatar seemed so innocuous, so innocent. The hopeful words of a young woman shared online between her and her friends. She shared the time. The date. The location.

"Oh my god. Are you saying she went missing in Roser Park?"

"Exactly. Someone is out here snatching girls up off the street." Emma threw up her arms. "I called and left a tip but who knows if they'll follow up. God, I wish I knew someone on the force..."

"Maybe it was an old boyfriend, or a stalker. She put her information out there. Anyone could have followed her."

"Or maybe this neighborhood is just fucked."

The sisters gasped as a loud vibrating noise punctuated the moment. Charlotte grabbed her buzzing phone and regarded the strange number on the caller ID. She gave Emma a strange look and answered the call. "Hello?"

"Charlotte! It's Judy! Sweetie, we just got your message!"

"Oh, hi." Charlotte exhaled. "I'm so glad you called."

"Listen, sweetie, we already called the vet's office. They're going to refund your card and get this all settled. I'm so glad Laurence is alright!"

Charlotte strained to listen as Judy continued to chatter away. Her voice was distant, and the connection wasn't clear. "Mrs. Collier, listen, I don't know if I can stay at the house any longer. Some strange things have been happening."

"Oh, nonsense! We'll be happy to pay you double for your troubles, just please stay. I'm going to have Adam rip out that damned plant once and for all, so you don't have to worry about Laurence getting into it again."

"Oh." Charlotte stammered. "Okay, but . . ."

"Charlotte, sweetie, our boat is going to board soon, but we'll call again when we're back on land. Goodbye now!"

The line went dead before Charlotte could protest further. She scoffed and glanced back up at Emma, her arms crossed at her chest and expression pale.

"Well?"

"They're going to reverse the charges of the vet

bill." Charlotte shrugged. "And they told me they'll pay me double if I stay."

"Fuck." Emma frowned.

A soft thud from the direction of the front sitting room caught their attention. Charlotte recognized it right away. The sound of a book hitting the floor.

"What was that?" Emma whispered.

"Mary." Charlotte grabbed her hand. "Come on."

Charlotte grabbed Emma's hand, let out a low, slow breath and turned toward the sound. She padded on the balls of her feet down the long, dark hallway to the front room with her sister close behind.

"Do you smell that?" Emma wrinkled her nose. "Like rotten roses."

Charlotte nodded and heard the faint swish of fabric. "That means she's here."

The front room was dark and still, left exactly as she had that morning. Mary's diary lay open on the floor in front of the couch in the same location she found her busted laptop only a few days earlier. Charlotte scooped up the book and began to read.

"Well? What does it say?" Emma said, her voice just above a whisper.

Charlotte choked on her own breath. Her throat burned as the contents of her stomach threatened to rise. She handed the diary to Emma and clasped a hand to her mouth. "It's worse than I thought."

Emma took the book from her, glanced down at the page under heavy brows and began to read.

Chapter Sixteen

Chapter Sixteen

Martin and his wife are sick, deranged people. I do not know how long I have been held against my will in this odd little room. I see the days pass outside, but I have lost track of the time. Has it been weeks? A month? I am their prisoner, but I do not have to wonder why. They readily tell me.

Martin's wife cannot have a child of her own. So, every evening after tea, I fall into a trance, though I am aware of what is happening to me. I still hear his hot breath in my ear, feel his weight against my body. It's only a matter of time before they are successful in their plan. They do not know that I have you here, Dear Diary. I fear that they will find it before I can gain enough strength to try and escape. I would run, but they've done something to my legs. I can't feel them anymore.

Perhaps I will see one of my little brothers playing in the yard next door and I can send them a signal. Perhaps father will come back from his business trip and care to check on me, his insane, unmarried daughter.

Or perhaps I will die here, a forgotten shell of who I used to be.

I dream of plunging the end of this pen into the soft folds of his neck. Then I'd do the same to his wife and set the sharp end deep into the back of her cold, careless eyes.

With every day, I lose less and less strength. I must reserve enough to escape. I do not know how they are getting away with this, how my family could be so near as I am tortured every day. I don't know if I'll ever see George again or feel the sand between my toes. There is only one thing that I know for sure; I will never allow my child to be raised by these vile, inhuman people.

I'd rather throw myself down the stairs.

Chapter Seventeen

Chapter Seventeen

"I'm going to be sick."

Emma held a hand to her mouth and leafed through the diary, rereading all the passages that Charlotte had already consumed. Charlotte was having a hard time keeping the contents of her stomach down herself. She glanced back up at the somber, silent face of Mary Mueller and finally understood.

"She wants us to tell her story." Charlotte took the diary from her sister. "That's gotta be it, right? This is her unfinished business."

"How awful." Emma hugged herself. "Um, okay. Shit, I guess I *do* have to start my own podcast. Wanna be my co-host?"

Charlotte chuckled. "Maybe."

The curtains moved ever so slightly, casting a long, triangular ray of golden light into the front room. Emma gasped and clasped her hands to her mouth again. For once, Charlotte's pulse didn't quicken. Instead, her thoughts became clearer than ever, and the voice called out to her again.

Look.

Charlotte followed the trail of light like an arrow to the edge of the couch where the carved wool area rug ended, and the original wood floor began. Something glinted and winked back at her in the ray of sun.

"Em, do you see that?" She kneeled by the couch, nearly in the area where her laptop and the diary had landed and peered under the couch. She plucked something small from behind the leg of the sofa and examined it in the palm of her hand.

"What is it?" Emma peered over her shoulder.

Charlotte picked up the mystery item in her hand. It was smooth and rounded on one side and jagged on the other. It had a plastic feel, and was painted in purple, black and white with a single jewel dotted at the end.

"Oh my god. Is that a . . ."

"It's a nail!" Charlotte shrieked and tossed the broken nail onto the couch like it was on fire. "Em, I'm gonna be sick."

Emma reached down and plucked the torn nail from between the cushions.

"I don't get it. It's gross, but maybe it was from the lady that lives here . . ."

The color drained from Charlotte's face. "No way. Judy is way too conservative to have acrylic nails like that."

"Well, there has to be another explanation."

Charlotte shook her head. "Also, I didn't tell you about the phone."

"What phone?"

"I found a pink flip phone buried in the couch. Like, an old one." Charlotte closed her eyes and sucked in a deep breath. "I told Adam about it. I thought maybe it was left over from some party one of the other house sitters had. But now, I'm not so sure."

"Okay, well are you sufficiently creeped out enough to leave now then?" Emma pulled her buzzing phone from her side pocket. "Hello?"

Charlotte glanced down at Laurence and then back up at Mary Mueller's portrait again. Her sister was right. It was time to trust her gut and go.

"Jesus, Brad. Okay, bye." Emma sighed and pinched her thumb and middle finger between the bridge of her nose. "Lacy is on her way to the ER. She fell during the game and hurt her wrist."

"Oh no!" Charlotte rose to follow her sister to the front door. "Is she okay?"

"Yeah, I just have the insurance cards and I need to go meet them there." Emma turned and pulled her into a hug. "I'm sorry, I've gotta go."

"That's okay. I'm going to pack my things and lock up here. I'll just get a cab to your place." Charlotte nodded. "You're right, it's not worth it to stay."

"Good. I'll tell Lacy you're bringing a dog over. That should cheer her up a little." Emma offered a weary smile. "It sucks to be a parent sometimes. No matter what you do, you never feel like you can protect them enough."

Charlotte watched as her sister bounded down the

walkway, her thoughts spinning in all directions. She turned toward the couch and her open duffel and plucked a sun dress from the bag. She pulled it over her still damp swimsuit, not even bothering to change. All she needed were her things and Laurence's crate and leash and she would be out the door. She would just return Laurence to Judy and Garret when they came back. She would...

BANG! BANG! BANG!

She sucked in a breath and turned toward the door. Laurence was already at the threshold whining, his tail flipping back and forth. She peered through the curtains and saw Adam waiting with a drink carrier on the other side. Charlotte rolled her eyes and answered the door.

"Hey, sorry. It's me again." Adam greeted her with his big, warm smile. He held out the drink carrier containing two to-go cups of coffee. "Um, I just wanted to come and apologize."

"Oh." Charlotte glanced down at the coffee cups and then back at him. "What for?"

"I don't think your sister is too fond of me." He chuckled and held up the coffee. "I also kind of barged in on you earlier. I thought I might try to make amends with caffeine."

"Are those from the cafe at the corner?" Charlotte eyed the familiar looking to-go cups.

"Yeah. I also got cream and sugars so you can make them the way you want."

She took the cup carrier and managed a smile.

"Thanks. That's really thoughtful. I still can't get the coffee to taste right here. I'm actually dying for caffeine."

"Good. Well, you have a nice night." Adam turned and paused, then turned back again. "And Charlotte. I'm really sorry if I came on too strong or gave mixed signals. I'll back off. But seriously, while you're here, please feel free to come by if you need anything."

Charlotte nodded, her eyes locking with his again. Was he just a nice neighbor or a shady ex-con? Or did the truth lie somewhere in the middle? She wasn't about to find out. "I'll remember. Thank you."

She waved and closed the door, taking the coffee with her. The smell of good quality dark roast wafted to her nose, and she took one of the warm cups in her hand. Coffee. Always a comfort in times like these. She took the cup with her and sipped as she secured the back door, turned out all the lights and rounded up Laurence's leash and food. She placed the last of her dishes in the dishwasher, emptied the trash and made sure the house was as neat and tidy as possible before texting her sister that she was on her way. All she had to do now was roundup the dog, call the car service and go.

"Laurence?" Charlotte's voice echoed through the house, now stiller and quieter than ever. "Sorry bud. I can't hang here. We gotta go."

The patter of nails sounded down the hall. Charlotte followed past the front living room and down the dark hallway toward the bathroom. She gasped as she entered the room. The corner closet door was wide open, only it wasn't a closet at all. She held her breath and padded into the bathroom, craning her neck to see. Instead of a hoard of toilet paper or antiques, the door gave way to a set of stairs. Somewhere down that staircase, Laurence yelped.

Oh fuck, oh fuck, oh fuck.

Charlotte's heart leapt from her throat as she approached the door. There was a modern looking light switch on the wall inside the door. Charlotte flicked it up and the darkened stairwell was bathed in warm light. The stairs were finished in new faux wood laminate and a handrail had been installed down the side. A basement.

Her head reeled as she ascended the first step in disbelief. No one in Florida had basements, it was almost unheard of. It hadn't even crossed her mind that the house could have one, and the Collier's certainly hadn't mentioned it. At that moment, it didn't matter to her if the ghost had opened the door or not. She just needed to get Laurence and get the hell out.

"Laurence! I'm coming!" Charlotte stepped down on increasingly wobbly legs. Her thoughts began to cloud. She needed to get out, to go. "Laurence!"

Finally, Charlotte reached the end of the staircase, her eyes heavy. She had reached a finished basement, designed to look like a cozy apartment. In one end of the room was a pair of recliners and a large television. Next to that was a small kitchenette with a hot plate and a mini refrigerator. Next to that was an unmade bed and a dresser. On the far end of the room was a cluster of monitors, each displaying real-time camera footage of the front of the house, the pool, the living room, the bathroom, and the kitchen. And there, at the helm of the command center, were Judy and Gary.

"Charlotte. Nice of you to join us." Gary clapped and stood from his rolling chair.

"What the fuck is this?" Charlotte wobbled back. She glanced over at Judy. Laurence perched on her lap as she stroked his fur.

"Well sweetie, this is our live feed. You're a little early, unfortunately." Charlotte blinked and backed up toward the stairs. "You've been filming me?"

"Yes. The buyers like to see their girl in action before they go up for auction." Garrett nodded. "Besides, you wouldn't believe how much we can charge for a subscription to our streaming platform."

"You're *sick*." Charlotte stumbled backward and fell into the stairs. Stars danced before her eyes as she clutched the rail and tried to pull herself up. The dank smell of decaying flowers grew more potent, filling her nostrils as he approached.

"No, we're *smart*."

The world grew hazy. Her legs and arms refused to work. Her eyes widened as Garrett reached for her hand.

"Sounds like you were about to get a little too smart too."

Chapter Eighteen

Chapter Eighteen
Charlotte awoke to the soft sound of rain. It was dark when her eyes fluttered open, and the air that surrounded her was still and musty. Her entire body ached as though she had fallen down a flight of stairs or been the victim of a car crash. Slowly, her thoughts cleared, and she became aware of where she was and why.

Her mouth was taped and tasted of plastic, her tongue dry and cottony. Her arms and legs were immobile, secured to the headboard and footboard with duct tape. A dull ache set into her temples, and after a terrifying moment, she realized where she was. It was in the upstairs room at the Roser Park house; the room that she was supposed to originally sleep in during her house-sitting gig. The very room that had creeped her out so much that she never wanted to set foot in there again. The room where Mary Mueller had been held captive more than a hundred years earlier.

Charlotte breathed heavily through her nose as she wriggled against her binds. Her lips pulled against the sticky mass of tape that sealed her mouth shut as she released a muffled scream. In one corner of the room a camera was trained on her bed, a red light indicating that it was on and likely filming her every move. Smatters of rain pelted the single square window framed by heavy curtains. A flash of lightning illuminated the room as she wriggled in her restraints, the tape at her wrists and ankles rubbing and burning against her skin. The harder she struggled, the more painful her ties became. Footsteps sounded down the stairs and her already elevated pulse quickened. A strip of light pierced through the dark and a man-shaped silhouette filled the doorway.

"Now, Charlotte, sweetheart. Don't get yourself all in a tizzy." She winced as Garrett flicked on the light and waved to the camera. He let out a deep sigh, pushed a button on the camera and rubbed the corner of his eyes before propping his hands on his hips. "You're gonna scare off the buyers with all of that wiggling and shaking."

Another set of footsteps sounded on the stairs. Charlotte's body went rigid and numb as Judy rounded the corner carrying a serving tray with a teapot and a matching teacup.

"My, you really do need a lot of this stuff to stay knocked out." Judy tsked, shook her head and laid the tray on the nightstand. "You know, I told Gary you were too old for this. Too old and too . . . *sturdy*."

"It's kind of a science, you see." Gary poured a steaming hot serving of tea into the cup. "The younger and more, well — *petite* — you are, the less you need. One cup and the other girls were out cold. But you? You're a tough cookie."

"That's why Laurence was out in an instant." Judy snapped her fingers. "He's actually our third Yorkie in the last five years. Turns out none of you are very good dog sitters."

Blood rushed to Charlotte's face as she struggled and shouted a muffled *fuck you*. Judy and Garrett chuckled in unison as he handed her the cup of tea. The couple were dressed just as she remembered; clean-cut, harmless looking carbon copies of each other in khaki and white. People like Judy and Garrett didn't do things like this. They were the kind of people that kept to their golf courses and craft stores. The kind of people that dined at buffets and took lavish vacations. They were owners of little dogs, keepers of a pristine garden. They could have been anyone's grandparents. Anyone's neighbor. How could they do this to her?

"Now I'm gonna hold your head still and Judy is gonna hold the cup and you're gonna drink this like a good girl." Garrett nodded. "Trust me, this is the easy way darlin'. Don't make it harder than it has to be."

Charlotte squeezed her eyes shut against a fresh crop of tears and clenched her jaw. She sobbed through her nose as Garrett placed his hands on her ears and made soft shushing sounds. Judy hovered over the bed with the teacup in her hand, gently re-moved the tape from her mouth and raised the cup to her lips. Charlotte allowed herself to take in half of the cup of warm tea, the familiar acrid taste that she never could quite place hitting the back of her tongue. She remained relaxed as she locked eyes with her captor, taking in every detail from the overwhelming floral scent of Judy's perfume to Garrett's soft, papery touch at her temples. Then as calm as could be, Charlotte spit the entire contents of her mouth in Judy's face.

"Oh, you little *bitch*!" Judy squealed and jumped back, the teacup flying through the air. The cup came down with a crash as she rose from the bed, arms flailing. Judy wiped at her eyes and growled. "You're lucky they pay less for damaged goods."

"Help!" Charlotte managed one loud yelp.

Garrett covered her mouth with the tape and sighed. "Well, I guess you want the hard way." He sighed and shook his head at the broken teacup. "What a mess."

Judy stormed out of the room and down the stairs, cursing all the way. Garrett followed at her heels, and Charlotte was alone once again. A loud rumble sounded overhead followed by the unmistakable crack of lightning and a dramatic flash of light outside. The storm was right on top of them. Charlotte's fight or flight senses were still in full effect as she struggled to listen to her captors bicker downstairs. In her panicked state, she tried her best to remain calm and think clearly. Surely, there was some way she could get out of this. Emma would come back soon and check on her. Adam would come knocking on the door and get suspicious. Someone would come looking for her. Or maybe not.

As she laid there trying not to panic, Charlotte's thoughts turned to Rochelle Davis. No one went looking for the pretty young college student except for her family and friends. In a moment of clarity, Charlotte realized that she had two choices. She could lay there, do nothing, and become another statistic. She would never get her nursing degree. Never make her own way in the world. Never see her nieces and nephew grow up. Or she could fight. She might die either way, but as a new burst of rage flowed through her veins, she knew which choice she would make.

A loud crack of thunder split through the air, practically rattling the shingles off the roof. The lights flickered, then the room fell into darkness. All at once, the hum of electricity and air conditioning quieted, and the house was still. Charlotte listened as Judy and Garrett bickered downstairs, arguing over where the candles and flashlights were kept. She didn't have much time.

Charlotte's hands were tied together with the same tape that covered her mouth, the binding rubbing and burning against her skin with every move. The tape over her mouth had just enough give from when she spit out the tea, and as a result, didn't have as secure of a seal as before. If she could only get the tape around her wrists wet somehow, she could break free.

A door slammed downstairs. Charlotte clenched her jaw and pulled her right arm against its binds.

She bit back a scream, the pain in her wrist searing into a blinding white heat as she closed her eyes and continued to pull. The flesh on her wrist began to rip away as she tugged and twisted at her arm. Hot tears streamed from her eyes as another flash of lightning filled the room, and for a brief moment, she could see a glint of something slick at her wrist. The tape was losing its grip on her shredded skin.

A burst of adrenaline and pure hope shot through Charlotte's veins as she continued to tug. She was numbing to the pain now, tugging and pulling with all her might to free her arm. She didn't have a plan beyond getting out of her restraints, but the hope of being free was all she needed to propel her. Finally, the tape made a soft squidgy *riiip* and Charlotte's right arm was free.

A triumphant, muffled laugh escaped from her throat as she began to claw at the tape on her left hand. Her right wrist throbbed as rivers of warm blood oozed from the raw, open flesh. She could barely feel anything, only thought to move, move, move as her numb fingers fought against the sticky tape. Then, the sound of footsteps on the stairs nearly stopped her heart.

She gasped and laid back in her bed, her heart hammering in her ears. Garrett whistled, his feet landing on the steps in ominous thuds as fingers of lightning tore through the night sky. Charlotte laid back and held her right arm over her head as he approached. In the flash of light, Charlotte's eye drew to the corner of the room. She blinked, unsure of what she had just seen, and then another bolt of lightning made her suspicions clear. There in the corner, standing still and silent as a statue, was a woman dressed in black.

"Looks like we have a little power outage on our hands." Garrett entered the room with a candle in one hand and a broom in the other. "Not to worry though. Judy is on the horn with the electric company right now. Should be back up in a jiff."

Garrett placed the candle on the nightstand and began to sweep up the broken teacup. Charlotte glanced toward the corner of the room, now able to see a little more clearly in the pale candlelight. The woman was gone. She remained still as possible while Garrett finished cleaning up, praying that he wouldn't notice her bloodied wrist. After what felt like an eternity, he was finally done sweeping.

"Be right back." He let out a low chuckle. "Don't go nowhere."

Charlotte let out a low, slow breath through her nose as he turned the corner and plodded back down the stairs. Her hand flew to the binds at her left wrist again, fingernails digging away at the tape. She was so focused on the task that she barely noticed the soft rustling of fabric, the eyes that always watched her. A tingling sensation danced up her spine and Charlotte knew she wasn't alone. She turned her head and gasped as a small, white hand crept along the side of the bed. The fingers were delicate and dainty, the nails perfectly polished into neat round ends.

Charlotte gazed down the length of the arm into a pair of dark, sad eyes; familiar eyes that she had studied so many times before set behind a curtain of strawberry blonde hair.

"Hi Mary." Charlotte's breath caught in her throat; the words muffled behind a layer of tape.

The specter smiled in recognition. She blinked and nodded; her somber expression just as beautiful in the candlelight as her image mounted over the fireplace. Then, before Charlotte could do or say anything, Mary dropped something on the bed and slipped into shadow.

"Wait!" Charlotte reached out as another flash of lightning filled the room and grasped nothing but air. Thunder shook the walls as she scanned the room, her breath hot and fast against the sticky, wet tape that now barely clung to her lips. She was alone again.

Judy and Garrett's voices floated up the stairs from the first floor and she knew she didn't have much more time. Her right hand fell to her side onto something long and smooth; the object Mary had dropped on the bed. She grasped the object and held it up to the candlelight. It was old and heavy with a pointed, sharp end. A fountain pen.

"You do it." Judy said, her stern voice sounding at the bottom of the stairs. "I need to go make another call; I don't have time for this."

Charlotte clutched the pen in her right hand, concentrating so as not to let it slip. Her palms were slick with blood, but still, she grasped the pen tight and returned her arm to its position against the headboard. Another flash of lightning illuminated the room as Garrett entered again, this time with a syringe. Her eyes opened wide as he held the needle up against the candlelight and tapped at the fluid inside the chamber.

"You know, they say that it isn't really necessary to tap at the chamber? It doesn't really push out any air bubbles." Garrett chuckled and moved to the side of the bed. "I don't know, I guess I just like to do it. Makes the whole thing feel a little more official."

Charlotte's body shuddered as he leaned over and pulled the blanket up from her legs.

"I'm gonna stick this right in your thigh, sweetheart." Garrett glanced back at her and his eyebrows knitted together. "You're gonna wanna be still or you'll just make it hurt worse."

Charlotte froze, breathing in slow and steady through her nose. The creases in Garrett's forehead deepened and the corners of his mouth turned down into a frown. He reached over and touched a dark spot on the bed.

"What in the world?" Garrett brought his hand into the candlelight and rubbed the pads of his thumb and middle finger together. Red glinted from his fingertips.

Charlotte's synapses fired on all cylinders as his eyes moved to her ruined hand. Garrett's confused expression fell into a dark, twisted grimace as he pieced together what she had done. Without thinking twice,

Charlotte brought the pen down and drove the sharp end into the soft folds of his neck.

Garrett's eyes and mouth opened wide as he clawed at himself, blood gushing in hot spurts from the open wound. Charlotte didn't wait for him to react. She drew her injured hand back and plunged the pen into his temple. He choked and gurgled, and the front of his immaculate polo shirt turned crimson as he fell to his knees. A warm sensation flooded into her lap as a stream of blood spilled from his neck and head. Garrett bobbled there for a moment, stunned and only able to grasp at himself, his eyes bulging as his formerly sun-tanned skin became ashen and gray. Finally, he slumped over the bed and slid to the floor, bringing the bloodied blanket down with him.

Charlotte went to work with the fountain pen as he expired, using the sharp end to tear at the tape on her left wrist and ankles. Finally free, she dropped the fountain pen, peeled the tape from her face and swung her legs off the side of the bed, her adrenal glands still working overtime. She tried to stand, but whether from being tied up for who knows how long or whatever drugs they had been giving her, Charlotte's knees buckled. She was running out of strength. She was losing her will.

Charlotte.

She braced herself on the bed and turned her head toward the voice. A black swish of skirt in the doorway. The scent of rotten flowers. Footsteps on the stairs. She pushed herself upright as another flash of lightning filled the room. Judy would be back any minute, and Charlotte was running out of time.

Chapter Nineteen

Chapter Nineteen
Charlotte had nowhere to run. Electricity coursed through the walls and the house hummed and clicked back to life. Just as quickly as it cut out, the power was restored again. She blinked against the bright light and stared down at her ruined wrist in disgust and disbelief. A strip of raw, angry flesh encircled her arm in flaps of skin stuck together with her already coagulating blood. If she were in any other situation Charlotte would wrap her wounds to stop the bleeding. But with Judy just around the corner, the only thing she had time for was to hide.

She tiptoed past Garrett's still and silent body, a lake of blood already spreading beneath him on the wooden floor. The fountain pen had been lost in the struggle somewhere, meaning Charlotte had nothing to defend herself with now but her wits. Her only hope would be to ambush Judy and run. Before she slid behind the door, her gaze fell again to something sharp and shiny at the foot of the bed. The syringe.

She bent down, grabbed the needle that was intended for her and slid behind the open bedroom door.

"Garrett, what the hell is taking so long?"

Judy's heavy footsteps sounded in the hall stopping just short at the doorway. Charlotte heard her gasp as the rubber soles of her sandals came screeching to a halt. Charlotte didn't wait to see what she would do next. She raised her bloodied arm up high and rounded the corner, not aiming for anywhere in particular. A roar escaped from her throat as she pounced from her hiding spot; a long-held scream, bottled up from years of frustration, suppression, and pain. It was a scream not only for herself, but for everyone else that came before her. A cry for all the Rochelle's and Mary's and Charlotte's of the world.

Her hand came down and the sharp end of the syringe pierced through Judy's cotton button-down and settled into the space where her heart should be. Charlotte used the last bit of her hand strength to plunge the contents of the syringe. She stepped back, shaking as Judy gasped. They both eyed the needle jutting out of her chest in a shared moment of shocked silence. Judy glared back up at Charlotte with cold eyes, her mouth screwed into a thin, gray line. She plucked the syringe from her chest and pulled her lips into a rictus grin.

"Sorry, sweetie. I've built up a tolerance. This stuff doesn't work on me."

Charlotte's eyes widened as Judy lunged at her, the end of the syringe held high. She was terrified, exhausted and injured. She had nowhere to run, nowhere to hide, but nothing would keep her in that room for another minute. With her last bit of bravery, Charlotte hunched over, ran at full force, and planted her shoulder into the soft center of Judy's stomach. A soft "oof" escaped Judy's lips as she made contact. Charlotte didn't stop pushing and running until her attacker was on the floor.

Judy landed with a heavy thud at the top of the stairs and let out a loud wail. Another rumble of thunder boomed overhead; this time much softer than before. The storm was winding down. Charlotte didn't wait for Judy to regain her footing and fled down the stairs. She didn't look back, only ran and ran as fast as her battered body could go.

Laurence greeted her at the foot of the stairs, a confused bundle of fur and nerves. He didn't seem to be too concerned for his masters and followed Charlotte down the dark, mirrored hall and into the front room. She paused for a moment as her hand curled around the front doorknob and glanced down at the little dog she had bonded with in such a short time. Laurence stared up at her with his expectant eyes. He didn't deserve to stay with these monsters either. Without thinking twice, she scooped him up with her good hand and opened the front door into the stormy night.

Rain whipped her face as she skittered down the walkway. Her feet were bare, and she didn't have her phone or money, or anything at all. There was really only one place she could go. One place where she would be safe. Where she and Laurence could hide until the cops came. She slid between the perfectly pruned hedges that cleaved the property line between the Mueller's and the Collier's houses and made a beeline for the front door.

"Adam!" Charlotte slammed her fist into the door again and again. Her throat was getting hoarse from screaming. She slapped the doorbell with her palm again and again and continued to scream just the same. "Adam!"

Her head spun, pulse racing as she glanced toward the darkened facade of the Collier's house. She half expected to see Judy coming up from behind with a butcher knife or a shotgun. Instead, the door swung open, and Adam greeted her with wide eyes.

"Oh my god. Charlotte."

She didn't wait for an invitation and pushed her way through, her pulse jackhammering away. Adam closed the door behind them and turned the deadbolt. Charlotte shuddered and backed into the front room, dripping rainwater and blood onto his floor. She clutched Laurence to her chest and struggled to catch her breath.

"It's Judy. She's trying to kill me!" She gasped, her voice coming out no more than a harsh whisper. "Please, you've gotta help me!"

"You're bleeding." Adam took off his plaid flannel and approached her.

She flinched and squeezed Laurence tighter. "I need to call the police."

"Yeah. I'll call them." He held his shirt out to her. "Here."

Charlotte nodded and took the shirt. She kept her eyes trained on Adam as she wrapped it around Laurence's shivering, wet little body.

Adam slipped his cell phone from his pants pocket and flinched. "You said Judy is trying to kill you?"

"Yes!" Charlotte hissed. "Please, just call them."

Her gaze darted around the room as he dialed, her breath and pulse finally slowing. Charlotte had never given much thought to what the interior of Adam's home would look like. Just like Collier's house it had that old home smell of wood and plaster and underlying rot. The layout of the front room was very similar, from the entryway and stairs to the left to the location of the fireplace in the front room. Adam's home was neat, tidy, and far more modern in decor than the Collier's house, with the exception of the oil painting hung over the fireplace mantle. A still life nature painting of a verdant green bush bursting with white angel trumpet blooms.

Yeah, I need an ambulance and an officer to come out to my home. My neighbor has been attacked." Adam spoke into the phone in a cool, collected voice and gazed up at her under heavy brows. "Yes. 682 Roser Park Drive. She's here."

Charlotte sucked in a shuddered breath. Laurence whined and trembled in her arms. She squeezed him and placed the damp little dog on a nearby recliner. The adrenaline in her system ran out and tears sprang from her eyes.

"Five minutes? Ok. Thank you." Adam ended the call and walked toward her. He held out his arms and she sank into his embrace. "Hey, it's ok. You're safe now."

A dry, choked cry escaped from her throat as she buried her face into his chest. She was certain that she was ruining his white shirt, but he didn't seem to mind. Charlotte squeezed her eyes tight against the tears and heaved as Adam stroked the back of her head. However, even as his arms encircled her, even as she breathed in his clean laundry scent and held her tight, she still didn't feel quite safe.

"They're monsters." She sobbed. "They were in the house the whole time, watching me."

"I don't understand." He held her tighter. "Judy and Gary? I thought they were on vacation?"

"*No*. They were hiding downstairs and filming me. I think they were drugging me with something." She pulled back and gazed up at Adam and his dark eyes. Her bloodied, battered hands clutched the thin fabric of his shirt as she steeled herself for the truth. "I killed Garrett. I had to."

"Oh no." Adam pulled her back into his embrace and pressed his lips into her forehead.

She winced and let out another long sob. "I think they were going to sell me or something."

"What?" Adam huffed. "How could they sell you?"

"I don't know." Charlotte wailed again. "Adam, I think they've done this to their other house sitters before."

"It's okay." He softly shushed her and cradled her face in his soft, warm hands. "The police will be here soon."

Charlotte shook her head and met his gaze. "It's not okay. It's so fucked up."

Adam leaned in and kissed her on the lips, soft and slow. He tasted of her tears and blood and something familiar that she couldn't quite place. At one time Charlotte had fantasized about that moment and what it would be like to feel the scruff of his cheek against her chin, his hands in her hair. The reality of kissing Adam Mueller was underwhelming. She didn't feel anything at all.

"Hey, let's go in the kitchen and get you settled down. You probably could use a drink before the cops get here."

She nodded and followed him on dead legs down the dark hall. A sick sensation crept up her spine as the footprint of the house continued to mirror the hellscape she had just run from. Laurence remained on the recliner, curled into a flannel ball and content to stay put. Like the house next door, the dark hallway led to the kitchen in a tight, claustrophobic pathway. However, unlike Judy and Garrett's modern kitchen, Adam's seemed to be still in its original state; cozy, dark and finished in wood and tile.

"Can I use your phone to call my sister?" Charlotte

hugged her arms to her chest. Even though her wrist had stopped bleeding, she would need medical attention soon. "I'm supposed to be at her house by now. I just want to call her and let her know what happened."

"Sure, there's a phone on the wall." Adam pointed to a phone that looked nearly as old as she was. A long, coiled extension cord was attached to the receiver, the kind of cord her mother used to drag all over the house behind her. "You want some coffee?"

"Sure." Charlotte picked up the receiver and dialed her sister's phone number, the only one she still knew by heart. She swallowed a lump in her throat as the line rang and went to voicemail. "Hey, Em. It's me. I'm going to be headed to the hospital soon. Something happened. I don't have my phone anymore. I just . . . I've been attacked. I'm next door right now, with Adam. I'm okay. Just . . . please, come out as soon as you get this, okay? I love you."

Charlotte let out a long, deep sigh and hung up the phone. Adam turned from the other side of the kitchen and pushed a hot cup of coffee into her hand.

"That was fast." She lifted the cup to her lips and took in a long, grateful sip.

"I always have coffee ready." He ran a hand through his hair. "I'm staying away from the hard stuff, so caffeine it is."

"We all have our vices." Charlotte leaned against the counter, her entire body humming as she drained the cup.

"So, Judy and Gary attacked you? I still can't believe it." Adam shoved his hands in his pockets. His keys jingled and he cleared his throat. "I always thought they were kind of odd, but I wouldn't think they were capable of something like *that*."

"They must run some kind of trafficking ring." Charlotte placed her cup on the kitchen counter. Across the way was a small, round dining table with four chairs. In the center of the table was a single vase filled with green leaves and white, bell-shaped flowers.

"And you think they were watching you?" Adam shifted on his feet and scratched the back of his head. "Man, I can't believe they were in the basement the whole time."

Charlotte's heart sped up. Her good hand shook as she gripped the coffee cup tighter. Her mouth was a desert again. Cotton. Sandpaper. She swallowed, shook her head, and forced herself to speak. "I never said they were in the basement."

Adam shrugged; the corner of his lips turned down into a half frown. "I guess I just assumed."

"Why would you assume that?" Charlotte glanced around the kitchen. Adam had all the essentials on his counter; a toaster, a coffee pot, even a stand designed just to hold bananas. But no knife block. Her pulse quickened.

"All of the houses in the neighborhood have base-ments. They're all raised up on a hill for the view and also to create a sub-level. It's one of the things that makes the development so unique."

Charlotte sucked in a deep breath and closed her eyes. Her head was light, her thoughts fuzzy. It was getting harder to think again.

"I'm just gonna call my sister one more time." She said, her voice shaky. "Maybe her husband will pick up this time."

"Sure." Adam took his phone from his pocket and began to tap at the screen.

Charlotte's eyes fluttered and struggled to open again as she reached for the phone. This time she dialed her own number. Laurence barked from the front room as the soft buzz of a silent cell phone ring vibrated somewhere nearby. She heard her own voice through the receiver. She sounded so far away. Her mouth tasted funny, and she was tired. So tired. Charlotte thought about Mary. About her sister. Her nieces. She thought about all the lost and forgotten people that couldn't be helped. She didn't want to meet the same fate.

"You never called the cops, did you?" Charlotte blinked, but her eyes were too heavy to open again this time. Her knees buckled and her legs gave out beneath her.

"Whoa, you need to sit down." Adam's arm slipped around her waist just in time to catch her. She stiffened at his touch, her arms slowly raising in a last-ditch attempt to shield herself. Charlotte forced her eyes open wide as he moved her to the kitchen chair.

A rainbow of light played on the ceiling just above his head as the scent of rotten flowers filled her nose and mouth.

Adam cradled her in his arms and glanced down at her, offering a warm, reassuring grin. "It's okay. You're safe."

She sank into the hard-back chair as a sick sensation slid into her gut. Charlotte didn't feel safe with Adam. Maybe she never actually did.

"What did you do to me?" Her voice came out slow, the words thick on her tongue.

"I'm sorry." Adam sighed. "I like you a lot, I really do. You're different from the other girls."

"Why?" She whispered.

"I owe Judy and Garrett. I can't let you ruin everything we've worked so hard to build." Adam ran his hand across her forehead, brushing the hair from her eyes. He smiled down at her warmly. "People are greedy and fucked up, Charlotte. Does there really have to be a why?"

It was then that a brilliant rainbow of light danced from the ceiling to a darkened corner of the kitchen and took a familiar shape. Adam's brows knitted together as he followed her gaze into the dark recesses of the kitchen. The color drained from his face as a pair of delicate, white hands reached out for him from the shadowy corner of the room.

"No." He shook his head and straightened, his fists balled up at his side.

The specter took full form then, more solid than

ever; more powerful somehow. Her eyes locked with Charlotte's and in that moment, their souls connected. Every last pain that Mary endured during her torture and entrapment was shared with Charlotte in that moment; every second of loneliness and agony - over a hundred years of loneliness. In that instance, Charlotte understood that Mary needed to be heard; her story needed to be told for her to take her power back. And take it, Mary would.

"This isn't real!" Adam shouted, stumbling backwards over a kitchen chair. "You're just some story my dad and Garrett made up! Some bullshit story!"

Mary locked eyes with Charlotte one last time, as if to ask for permission. Charlotte used her last ounce of energy to nod in understanding.

"Do it."

The last thing Charlotte remembered was Mary unfolding her milky arms and embracing her with dark eyes shining and teeth sharp and bright. Charlotte closed her heavy eyes and allowed Mary to embody her. Together, they enacted her revenge with Charlotte only a mere passenger. She felt nothing as Adam screamed under her spirit-guided hand until his voice became nothing more than a choked sputter. And then, as soon as it began, the job was done. Mary's spirit left her body and Charlotte tumbled to the floor and knew darkness and nothing more.

Chapter Twenty

Chapter Twenty

Charlotte awoke to a warm, wet sensation on her cheek and the muffled sound of banging. She groaned, her entire body slow to come to life, wrists aching and a hangover headache in full effect. She opened her heavy eyelids to see a sweet, furry muzzle and a pink tongue.

"I don't give a shit! I know she's in there! Charlotte!" Emma's muffled voice sounded through the haze, followed by more banging.

Charlotte forced herself into an upright position and glanced around Adam's kitchen. His body was sprawled out on the opposite end of the room, silent and still. A puddle of coagulated red encircled his head like a grisly halo. Laurence whined and licked the wounds on her wrist and everything started to become a little more clear. A cracking noise followed by more bangs and the creak of hinges sounded from the front of the house.

"Charlotte! Are you in here!"

"Back here!" Charlotte coughed, scooped Laurence up and stood to her feet.

"Oh, thank goodness!" Emma appeared seconds later, her face stricken and pale. She wrapped Charlotte into a tight hug as a sob shuddered through her body. "I thought I had lost you."

"I tried to call you." Charlotte said, the words still heavy and slow on her tongue. "Those bastards were drugging me."

"Oh my god. I'm so sorry." Emma squeezed her tighter, glanced over her shoulder at Adam's lifeless form and gasped. "Did you kill him?"

"No. The ghost did that." Charlotte said. "I tried to call you..."

Before she could explain herself any further, a half dozen police officers spilled into the house.

"I found her! See! I told you she was in here!" Emma glared at them, her arms still wrapped protectively around Charlotte.

The house thundered with the sound of a dozen boots against the hardwood floor. A blonde, petite officer turned the corner into the kitchen.

"M'am, you can't just break into..." The officer's eyes grew wide as she took in the kitchen scene, her gaze fixed on Adam's body. She called over her shoulder and reached for her weapon. "Hey, we got a possible 187 back here!"

***

"Would you like a ride to the station, Miss. Slater?" Officer Jennifer Hardy handed Charlotte a business card with her case number on it. "We just need to get an official statement down at the station."

Charlotte had spent the past hour being interviewed by detectives, photographed and examined by emergency medical technicians. Journalists showed up shortly thereafter, but Emma was quick to tell the press to back off. A half dozen police cars lined Roser Park Drive, bathing the neighborhood in blue and red light. Yellow tape had already been strung up along the Collier's house and Adam's house as a handful of detectives moved about the property taking notes and photographs. A few nosy neighbors stood in their driveways or at a safe distance across the street to try and get a good look at the commotion.

Charlotte took the business card and pulled her emergency blanket around her shoulders. The dressing on her wrist from the medical technician was tight and fresh.

"I'm going to see that she gets to the hospital first." Emma sneered at the officer and folded her arms at her chest.

"Understandable." Officer Hardy tipped her cap. "Y'all take care now."

"You too." Emma huffed and rolled her eyes.

"Great."

"Idiots." Emma said under her breath.

"So what now?" Charlotte chuckled and thumbed the business card.

"Now, we get you to the hospital and make sure those psychos didn't do any real damage to you."

"How did you know where to find me?" Charlotte glanced up at Emma under a heavy brow.

"Intuition, I guess." Emma shrugged. "I couldn't find my phone when I got to the hospital, so I borrowed Brad's and tried to call you. You didn't pick up, and I just knew something was wrong. Then when some lady answered the door and tried to tell me that you left town, I knew right away that I needed to call the cops."

"Judy." Charlotte let out a bitter chuckle. "What a bitch."

"You should have seen her face when the cops showed up." Emma shook her head. "It was really satisfying to see her in handcuffs though. Why do rich people think they can get away with anything?"

"Because rich people always get away with things." A tremor wracked through Charlotte's body. Rochelle. Mary. Countless others. How many more people would have suffered because of them? And Adam... perhaps his involvement was what hurt most of all.

"How is Lacy?"

"She's fine. They put a cast on her wrist." Emma's voice cracked. "I just can't believe all this happened."

"I can." Charlotte glanced up toward the twin Roser Park homes with disgust. "Humans are awful to each other sometimes."

"Not all the time." Emma sighed and gave her a weak smile. "Are you sure you don't want to take the ambulance?"

"Nah. It's too expensive." Charlotte shrugged. "Besides, the hospital is only a mile away."

"Okay. Let's go get you checked out then."

Charlotte shivered and followed Emma to her van. "So do you think I'll go to jail?"

"I don't see how." Emma unlocked her van and opened the driver's side door. "There's plenty of evidence that you acted in self-defense. Just don't tell them the truth."

"The truth? That a ghost helped me kill my attackers and get away?" Charlotte scoffed. "Yeah, no thanks. I definitely don't need that kind of attention."

Charlotte slipped into the safety of her sister's van, comforted by the familiar smell of stale apple juice and vanilla air freshener. Laurence yipped from the back seat and hopped onto the console. In the commotion, Emma had thought to scoop him up and leave him in the van with the windows cracked.

"There he is." Charlotte cooed and buried her face into the dog's neck. "They can't hurt you anymore either, bud."

"How the heck am I gonna get out of here?" Emma turned over the ignition and rolled down her window and shouted. "Hey move! I need to get this lady to the hospital!"

Reporters and gawkers jumped and quickly cleared out of the road. Emma turned onto Roser Park Drive away from the scene of the crime for what Charlotte hoped would be the last time. Laurence whined and his little body trembled as he pawed at the passenger side window.

"It's okay, bud. It's over now."

Charlotte followed his gaze toward the darkened, tree-lined waters of Booker Creek. Two hazy figures stood out in the dark of night, bathed in a soft, other-wordly glow. Charlotte's breath hitched in her throat as the spirit of Mary glanced over her shoulder and joined hands with the glowing spirit of a man. She smiled and waved as Charlotte and Emma drove away from Roser Park.

"You're free now." Charlotte pressed her fingertips to her lips and blew the figures a kiss. She whipped her head around to get a better look at them as they passed, but all she could see was flashing red and blue lights in the rearview.

It wasn't over; not for Charlotte, not really. Not by a long-shot. There would be plenty of medical and probably psychological tests in her future. Visits with licensed therapists and counselors, followed by what she hoped would be a swift trial. But as they turned away from the suburbs and back toward downtown, Charlotte knew that her brief stay at Roser Park would always be with her somehow. On dark, lonely nights she would close her eyes and see the ghoulish faces of her captors. Dating would be hard, maybe impossible for a long time. She was going to need a lot of therapy to trust again. But she was safe, and Mary was free, and soon the truth would come to light about what happened at 684 Roser Park Drive.

"Did you say something?" Emma glanced over at her in the darkened cab. Even in the low light, Charlotte could recognize the look of concern on her sister's face.

"Oh, nothing. I'm just glad we have Laurence." Charlotte hugged the dog tighter to her chest, and finally her shoulders relaxed.

"Me too." Emma gave him a scratch. "He's a good boy."

"The best."

Emma yawned. "I don't know about you, but I could use a cup of coffee."

"Not me. No thank you." Charlotte laughed, a low, dark chuckle. "I was thinking maybe we should do that true crime podcast after all. The Roser Park Files."

"Don't tempt me." Emma said, her concerned, tired expression sliding into a smile. "But seriously, I have all of the equipment if you want to give it a go."

"We'll see."

"There's still a lot of unanswered questions," Emma continued. "Like Adam! What a creeper. I *knew* he was a creep..."

"Not *all* criminals are creeps." Charlotte nuzzled Laurence again.

"But this one was!"

"Yeah. You're right." Charlotte sighed. "I should have trusted you. I should have trusted my instincts."

"*Always* trust your instincts." Emma said, checking her rearview. "Oh, there's the exit."

The brightly lit sign for Bayfront Hospital came

into view and Charlotte closed her eyes, allowing the rocking motions of the van to lull her. Her body ached and was numb all at once, and even though she felt safe for the moment, Charlotte knew that the worst was yet to come. Nightmares. Flashbacks. She was familiar with it all. The fight wasn't over yet, but this time, Charlotte was going to stand tall. Even though her body and her spirit felt broken, there were still so many mysteries to uncover. Still so many families of missing people that needed answers and justice and peace. Justice would be served in time, but for now, Charlotte was safe and grateful to be alive, thanks to the love of a nosy little sister, a ghost named Mary, and a sweet little dog named Laurence.

Wendy Dalrymple loves to explore the beauty in horrific things. When she's not writing Florida Gothic horror or romantic thrillers, you can find her hiking with her family, painting (bad) wall art, and trying to grow as many pineapples as possible.

Keep up with Wendy at www.wendydalrymple.com or follow her on Twitter @wendy_dalrymple.

Printed in the USA
CPSIA information can be obtained
at www.ICGtesting.com
LVHW091251271123
764762LV00059B/2101

9 798218 089955